The Fifth Son

The Fifth Son

Blaine D. Arden

Illustrated by Yana Goya

The Fifth Son
Copyright © 2012 Blaine D. Arden
ISBN: 978-90-822966-0-0
Paperback edition - Printed by CreateSpace

Cover Art by Simoné. www.dreamarian.com
Illustrations by Yana Goya
Edited by KJ Charles
Proofread by Tami Veldura
Layout by Cayendi Press

Second Edition - November 2014
First Edition - March 2012 (Storm Moon Press)

Cayendi Press
Zutphen
The Netherlands
CPress@cayendi.nl

Also available in ebook
ISBN: 978-90-822966-1-7

To Mum
(1947-1994)

Table of Contents

Chapter One

I T STARTED WITH a line, just one line. Before long, the line became a brushstroke, a smear, a shape. Once I started with that single line, I could not stop. I needed to capture every detail, every hint of movement—from the biggest tree to the tiniest flower, to the way the leaves shuddered in the wind—every glimmer and shadow. Whether brush or pencil, canvas or pad, I had to keep painting until that first line had become a finished work, no matter how long it would take.

Which was how I found myself standing at the edge of the waterfall in the fast-fading sunlight.

The bells announcing the end of the midday break had not yet stopped ringing when I arrived at my favourite spot some hours ago. The rays of sun hit the waterfall at just the right angle, creating a beautiful play of shadows as the water crashed into the shaded fen, spraying drops of light everywhere. I spent hours trying to recreate those shadows, the sparkling water, and the way it all moved. The changing light made it difficult, but that first image was so clear in my mind that I hardly had to look up from my work. Surrounded by the thundering sounds of the waterfall and the smells of fresh water, tangy hindra bushes, and sweet yellow nara flowers, I worked until I had put the last bit of shade in, and my painting was done.

I should have gone home then, but I had barely wrapped the painting when the water nymphs came out to play. They must have known I was there, but they splashed around as if I wasn't, their lithe figures almost floating on the surface. I had never seen them so joyous, and I couldn't resist grabbing a new canvas to paint them, losing track of time in the process.

With one last look at the water nymphs, I hoisted my bags onto my shoulders and made my way down the path leading to the castle grounds. I would have to hurry. It would be dark soon, and Father would be furious if he found out I had sneaked off without my guard. Again.

He had warned me over and over not to stray too far and to always take Neia with me. But, painting with someone constantly watching me wasn't easy. Neia tried to keep her distance, but I still felt her eyes on me all the time. I itched to be alone. Not alone in my room. No, alone out here, painting without being disturbed or being told when to go home.

I had tricked Neia into believing I would be in town all day with Endyrr, one of my brothers, visiting his lover, Kalnor. Endyrr and Kalnor would believe I had been at the castle since midday, because they had accompanied me back to the outer gardens then. It had been easy to grab my leather painting bags from their hiding place in the hedge, and walk out again after my companions had disappeared from view. With no one working in the gardens around midday, there had been no danger of being seen.

My crunching steps sounded loud in the otherwise quiet forest; I could barely hear the waterfall over their noise. I kept my eyes on the ground in front of me, avoiding thorns and poison creepers as best as I could, and stepping over any stumps and branches in my way. I should have taken the path: it was wider and there were fewer obstacles to trip over in this fading light. But this way I would reach the castle grounds sooner, and hopefully before anyone realised I wasn't where they thought I was.

Leaves rustled behind me, and I froze. I hoped it was one of the castle's cats out hunting and not a boar smelling dinner, but I still changed my grip on the bag holding my paints and palette. It was heavy enough to hit a boar with, surely. Not that I thought of doing so—I had been taught to be as still as possible when the boars were around—but if it moved in on me, I would have to fight. I had no hope of outrunning one.

A twig snapped, in front of me this time, and I closed my eyes.

"Don't move."

I sighed as I recognised Captain Ariv's deep, gravelly voice, torn between relief at having one of Father's men save me from a boar, and annoyance at being caught off grounds.

Something shiny caught my eye, but before I could react to it, I heard the familiar zing of a shooter, and whatever was behind me dropped with a low-pitched whine. The ground trembled beneath my feet, but when I looked back, I saw nothing. The beast was probably hidden by the hindra bushes.

"Come. That boar'll stay down long enough for us to get out of here."

I faced the captain, only to discover his shooter aimed at me. No, not at me, at the boar, but that didn't matter. The shooter was right in my line of sight, the way it always happened in my fantasies. The copper shooter glinted in the barest hint of light, and I shivered as I caught a whiff of lingering magic amongst the tangy smell of the hindra bushes.

The hand holding the shooter was large and strong, a perfect fit around the shooter's handle. I was painfully aware of the captain's presence, and I swallowed the moan threatening to escape as I resisted the urge to adjust my trousers, covered by my, thankfully, loose-fitting tunic. Instead, I tried to take deep breaths that kept ending in gasps and did nothing to stop my body responding as if to a lover's touch. I wanted to look away, but couldn't. How I longed to feel the effects of a stunning spell, wanted that strong hand to tense around the handle, to...

I bit my lip to keep from making a sound and moved my bags in front of me, hoping Captain Ariv hadn't noticed my reaction. I needed to look away, needed to walk on, but I couldn't make myself. I was frozen. Again. Only this time it had nothing to do with fear.

When Captain Ariv finally lowered his shooter, my head bowed with it, my eyes following its descent until it disappeared behind his back. I sighed.

"Your Highness? What are you doing out here?"

I forced myself to look up at him, showed him my bags, and aimed for a smile.

Captain Ariv frowned. "You're not supposed to—"

"Stray off the grounds on my own. I know," I interrupted him, ignoring the slight wobble in my voice. "I lost track of time."

"And Neia?"

Ouch. There was that. The story of my life. The fifth son of the king of Eizyrr, the powerless one who needed constant supervision, the one who could never fight for his kingdom. No doubt I'd be the talk of the soldiers tomorrow. *"Found wandering outside the castle grounds again,"* they'd say, *"on his own, without his guard, and retrieved like a stubborn little puppy."* I barely kept from balling my fists around the straps of my bags. I wasn't a stripling any more. "D'you think you can take me to my rooms, Captain?" I said as calmly as I could manage.

For a moment he just stared at me, eyes narrowed, as if trying to see into me. Then he grinned, a wide grin that made me wonder if he was up to something.

"Of course, Your Highness. I take it you don't want the king to know?"

I doubted that was possible, but I nodded anyway.

"Well, then, Your Highness. Let me carry that for you, and I'll sneak you past the guards."

I almost refused, but if he wanted to carry my bags for me, so be it. He seemed surprised at their weight as he took them, yet hefted them both onto one shoulder without effort and turned around, clearly expecting me to follow him. Was he really going to help me get past the guards? Probably not, but it was nice to think he was.

I looked behind me and thought of the water nymphs. I hoped I wouldn't be grounded for long.

NEARING THE OUTER walls, I could hardly even see the battlements of the castle. I could see the four towers, though, their roofs as green as the vines covering the dark grey stone walls.

Although he'd told me otherwise, I expected Captain Ariv to march me straight through the gate to Father. Instead, he left me standing in the shadows as he chatted amiably with the guards, distracting them so I could pass by unseen, and did the same at the inner walls. Apparently, he was a man of his word.

Out of habit, I stopped halfway into the gardens, and looked up at the castle. If anyone saw me out here now, they would think I had just arrived back from town, provided Captain Ariv didn't tell on me. I watched the flickering lanterns lighting up the high, dark walls in an eerie mix of greens and greys, broken only by wavering hues of yellow from the lamps burning in the windows. I had painted the castle like this once.

Mother hung it in the dining room, the private one.

There were no lights coming from my tower, barring the lamp I put on the hall table in the morning. The rest were hidden away in cupboards. I used to leave them out, but their artificial glow ruined the wondrous shapes daylight created on my walls. I hated those lamps, hated having to ask others to turn them off, but Mother did not trust me with candles, not when I couldn't douse them with magic. Her refusal to acknowledge that candles didn't need magic always baffled me.

I sauntered towards my tower, containing the only magicless rooms in the castle, not counting the lamps. They hadn't always been so, but when I kept bumping into the doors, got my fingers caught, and even got stuck in the bathroom once, they had been rebuilt without magic. Now others bumped into my doors when they forgot.

Neia's room, at the bottom of the stairs, was empty. Relieved not to have to explain myself to her, I climbed the stairs and let myself in, taking the lamp with me. My walls lit up as I placed more lamps around the room. I smiled, remembering the tantrums I had thrown when my parents refused to repaint my walls. Even at six, I had been very picky about my colours. In the end they had given in to my wishes, though it had taken three tries to get a green that would look like a hint of fresh moss in daylight, but wouldn't turn the colour of a budgerigar at night. I reached for my bags, only to realise Captain Ariv still had them. Now I'd have to go all the way to the northern walls, to the captains' quarters, to get them back. But when I opened my door, Captain Ariv stood in the hall with that wide grin on his face, holding out my bags.

"You forgot these, Your Highness."

"Yes, thank you, Captain." I reached for the bags.

"May I see your paintings?"

I opened my mouth and closed it. It wasn't as if I hadn't

entertained anyone in my rooms before, though never one of Father's men, and certainly never someone as formidable, as desirable, as Captain Ariv. I looked behind me. My desk, a chunky dark brown piece of wood, was strewn with brushes, pencils and drawing pads, both new and filled with sketches, but the rest seemed presentable. I moved aside to let him in.

Captain Ariv looked around as I closed the door. He walked over to my desk and put the bag of paints down on the floor next to it. I followed him and reached for the other bag, but he ignored me and started unpacking it himself. He took his time, too, studying both paintings as he unwrapped them, putting the one with the water nymphs on the easel, and the one with the waterfall on my desk. He stepped back and studied them. "You make them come alive."

I shook my head. "They are alive. I merely paint them as they are."

His expression turned thoughtful, and a shiver crawled up my spine. "Let me see your work."

I frowned. "My work can be seen all around the castle."

"The ones you don't show."

I stared at him, my heart thumping, hoping I had misunderstood.

I was tall, but still had to look up to him, and he was much broader than my wiry frame. Then again, everyone was broader than I would ever be. They said I looked like my mother, with my grey eyes and long hair as red as the kozal roses, but even she was more muscular than I was. Bloody magic.

Captain Ariv's eyes were darker than any I'd ever seen. They had to be brown, but they were so dark they looked black, as black as his spiky hair. Black, yet not cold, even though they seemed to stare straight through me, intent, yet thoughtful. I had to fight not to lick my lips. His presence stirred me, almost as much as his shooter had. I closed my eyes at the memory and swallowed, willing myself not to become hard.

He caressed my cheek. It would be so easy to lean into his touch. His hand stilled and moved away. I opened my eyes to find him standing at the door, watching me and shaking his head. "Go to sleep, your Highness. And do not go off grounds without Neia again." He slipped out of my room.

I took a shaky breath and leaned against my desk, watching the closed door. What had just happened? How had he known about *those* paintings?

Unsteady on my feet, my steps heavy and clunky, I ascended the stairs and walked through my bedroom into my private gallery, closing the door behind me. I sank down on the bench in the middle of the room and stared at the painting in front of me. I hadn't known his name when I first painted him, but now I easily recognised the hand I'd seen up close in the forest. It was beautiful. *He* was beautiful. His expression had been serious when I painted him. A bit younger, his hair sticking out to all sides, eyes half closed in the bright sunlight, squinting at something to my left.

I had never seen him smile on the training field, yet he was not a cruel man. He fought fair, fought clever, never seemed excessively hurtful—even though he was probably one of the strongest men out there—and wielded the shooter with skill. I looked away from his face to what made me paint him that day. The copper of his shooter reflected bright rays of sun. His hand seemed less tanned and the position was not quite the same, but my pulse raced nonetheless.

My eyes glued to the shooter, I laid back and freed my cock, running my fingers up and down as I imagined my body yielding to the stunning spell. I imagined another's hand, Captain Ariv's hand, jacking me off hard and fast as I lay stunned, and bit my lip to keep from crying out as I came.

Chapter Two

HOLDING MY FISTS in front of me, ignoring the sweat trickling down my neck and forehead, I moved around the dummy, balancing on the balls of my feet. I kept my eye on it, pretending it was attacking me and I needed one good hit to knock it down. I struck out with my right, quickly following it with my left, keeping my balance as I fell into a rhythm. Left, right, left, left, right, left, right, right. I pushed all my frustration into it as I hit the dummy again and again.

Captain Ariv had not told Father about me sneaking off grounds, and I had heard no rumours amongst the soldiers, either. I didn't know whether to be thankful or frustrated.

Still, I had played it safe and barely left the castle grounds all week—well, not without Neia and not after dark—and now I was itching to be alone again, to be free from being guarded. Which was why I stretched my morning workout as far as I could, while Neia dutifully stood outside the door of the training hall.

It felt so good to hit the dummy. Some days I even pretended it was Captain Ariv, although hitting him was the last thing I wanted to do. I lost a beat as I thought about how I'd brought myself off almost every night this past week, fantasising about Captain Ariv. It didn't matter whether Captain Ariv or other soldiers featured in my shooter paintings, they all stirred me in the same way, but I couldn't stop picturing *him* as I came, his dark brown eyes trained on me with that intense expression and that wide grin of his. He was gorgeous.

"You need to raise your left hand, Your Highness."

At the sound of Captain Ariv's voice, the punch I was throwing went wild. I missed the dummy altogether, stumbled, and only kept myself from falling face first to the floor by grabbing it. I pushed myself upright and turned towards Captain Ariv, but could barely bring myself to look at him.

He came up to me, grabbed my fists and put them in position, evidently unaware of my heart pounding in my chest. "Try again."

I did, trying to regain my composure.

"No, stay in one place. You need to get your arms in the right position first."

I stopped, took a breath, raised my hands again, and punched. Left, right, right, left.

"Raise the left, you keep dropping it."

I raised my left and punched, going through the sequence of hits again, and again. Somehow not having to look at him made it easier to focus, to forget who he was.

"Better. Can you feel the difference?"

At first, I wasn't sure what he meant by feeling the difference, but as I kept punching, kept checking the position of my hands, my rhythm changed. It smoothed out, and my punches became tighter. I nodded.

"Good. Keep it up."

I kept punching until my mouth went dry and sweat started irritating my eyes. Taking deep breaths, I wiped the sweat off my forehead and. My hands felt like rocks as I lowered them. I could no longer avoid looking at Captain Ariv,

and, of course, he was watching me with *that* grin on his face.

"You have a good technique, Your Highness. Did your brothers teach you?"

I snorted. "I've watched field trainings since I was little, I was bound to pick up something." No need to mention that my brothers weren't allowed to fight me; that *I* wasn't allowed to fight. No magic, no soldier, no training.

"You are allowed to work out in here?"

"Yes." Never with a sparring partner, though. My parents didn't want me to get hurt.

Captain Ariv frowned but said nothing. He looked as sweaty as I felt. He must have just finished his morning training.

"Did you need anything?" I asked, watching a droplet trickle down the side of his face. I wanted to lick it off. I looked away.

"Go take a shower. You don't have much time before the company arrives," he said and turned to leave. "Good work, Your Highness."

Compliments from Captain Ariv. I must not be too bad at this. Or was he just indulging me?

I hurried into the shower, letting the water soothe my sore muscles and calm my mind, if only enough to stop me from doing something stupid like jacking off in these communal showers.

Fortunately, nothing, no one, stopped me from taking refuge in my gallery to do just that. I sank down on the bench, naked, and took the shooter from its hiding place underneath. It did nothing for me. My palms didn't go sweaty when I held it, my cock stayed soft, and my breathing never changed.

I remembered how thrilled I had been, the day I managed to get my hands on it. Someone had thrown it away, broken beyond repair. I couldn't make it work even if it wasn't broken, so that hadn't mattered. I had been convinced that even a broken shooter would soothe my dreams, my desires. But possessing one just wasn't the same. It would never be the same.

Still, I couldn't resist trailing it over my chest, my stomach, and the insides of my legs as I pleasured myself, staring at Captain Ariv in the paintings, the sketches, old and new. I had moved them all to one side now, wanting to see only him aiming his shooter at me. He never was, of course, but I was good at pretending. Good enough that my muscles tensed under the influence of an imaginary stunning spell, and I only had to close my eyes to imagine the accompanying whiff of magic lingering in the humid air of my gallery.

I came too fast, too soon, leaving me empty and unsatisfied.

This would not do. Not any more.

Captain Ariv did not appear in the training hall the next few mornings, foiling my no doubt ill-thought plan to seduce him there, but I didn't let that ruin my newly found determination. So, I packed my painting bags and made my way to the training fields, with Neia following me closely.

The field was doused in sunlight, drifting dry sand, and sweaty soldiers practising their swordplay and stick fighting. I managed to find a spot in the shade, away from the blowing sand. I started with a bit of sketching first. The soldiers closest to me fought with sticks—long ones, short ones, single and double. I sketched their poses, their hits, their misses, feeling the ground tremble beneath me as the practising became more aggressive. By the time I finished the last of my sketches, my throat was dry, despite sitting away from the sand-blowing wind, and my voice was scratchy as I asked Neia for some water. The soldiers, while sweaty, hardly seemed tired. Training was far from over.

I put a canvas on my easel and looked around the field, sipping my water, searching for an appealing object to paint. Captain Ariv wasn't training, himself; he was supervising a group on the other side of the field in hand-to-hand combat. Still, I could not help staring at him and the way his skin glistened in the sunshine.

"Ogling the men, Llyskel? Seems like you found the perfect spot for it."

Kalnor stood behind me, long blond hair falling in his eyes as he looked down at me.

"Kalnor. Good to see you." I smiled at him and patted the ground. "Sit. You can join me for a moment, can't you? I'm sure your siblings won't mind."

"If it means ogling my beloved Endyrr a little longer, I'm game." Kalnor sat down beside me. "My siblings be damned."

We both gazed across the field, to where Endyrr swung his long stick about with ease, holding off his attacker, while explaining his moves to his group.

Kalnor sighed. "I could watch him at this all day."

I looked from Endyrr to Kalnor and knew I had my model. It had been a while since I had painted any of my brothers. I was about to tell him when a high-pitched screaming interrupted our conversation. We both turned our heads to the row of orrin bushes across from the entrance in the garden wall. I didn't see Sirr or Inau, but Neia had already raised a shield to block any stray magic coming from my frustrated little niece, who must have escaped her mother. I smiled at Neia, mouthing my thanks, and hoped Sirr was still within the inner walls and nowhere near the training fields.

"How long has Sirr been volatile?" Kalnor asked.

"About a week, I think." A long week in which I hadn't

even caught a glimpse of her. She usually enticed me to play marbles with her at least once a day, or joined me as I painted, creating her own art with her colouring sticks or old brushes I saved for her. "She already hurt two of the kitchen staff because they weren't shielding themselves properly."

"So, you're allowed nowhere near her, I take it?"

"I'm not allowed anywhere near the annex at the west wall, which is where Danen and Inau have moved for the time being. And Sirr is not allowed in the castle or past that row of orin bushes. I guess it's a fair trade-off."

"Nothing as dangerous as a child coming into their powers. Mother said I nearly burnt the house down."

I still remembered the look on my parents' faces when they realised I would never come into my powers. I envied Sirr, tantrums and all. And I missed playing with her.

As I turned back to the training field. Endyrr's group had moved closer and switched to swords. Perfect. No doubt Kalnor would very much like to have a painting of Endyrr with his sword in his workshop.

Kalnor got up and dusted off his leather work tunic and trousers. "If I want to meet Endyrr for dinner tonight, I'd best get back to work."

I nodded and wished him well, never taking my eyes off Endyrr. I grabbed my brush and my palette and studied the way he moved, the way he raised his brow when his opponent made a mistake, the way he held his shield. I barely noticed I had started the first lines even before I decided on the pose. Endyrr moving around made it difficult to choose, but when I found a pose I liked, it didn't matter that he wouldn't stand still. Once I had that image in my head, the painting would almost paint itself. I copied the pose of Endyrr with his sword slightly raised, shield hip high, and his face in full sunlight. Maybe I could surprise Kalnor by delivering the painting to his workshop later this week. I enjoyed walking into town, even with Neia trailing after me.

Sirr's screaming stopped at last. I turned my head to check on Neia, who slumped as she released her shield. She immediately started a relaxation exercise, because holding up a shield for that long took its toll. I sighed. Neia was just doing her job, and I often treated her as if she was unwanted. Maybe she would like a painting of her own.

The ground shook as something hit it with a loud thump, and I turned back to watch the soldiers. The soldier training with Endyrr had gone down. I would paint Neia another day. Today was Endyrr's turn.

Endyrr leaned on his sword, panting, but only until the next soldier took his place before him. This one attacked at once, and then ducked behind Endyrr. How he could even sense where his opponent was, I had no idea, but Endyrr did not have any trouble fighting him off and forcing him back.

By the time I moved on to sketching the background, Endyrr had long stopped fighting and was now merely instructing his soldiers as they practised their moves. I put my tools down for a moment and gratefully took the water Neia handed me, gulping it down as I searched the field for a moment, but Captain Ariv was nowhere to be found. Perhaps he had taken his soldiers on a run.

"Kalnor will no doubt love the pose."

Captain Ariv's voice washed over me, and I was glad to have drained my cup already, I would have ruined the painting otherwise.

He looked down into my face with that wide grin plastered on. "I'm sorry, Your Highness. I didn't mean to startle you."

I narrowed my eyes. If I didn't know any better, I'd say he was doing it on purpose, but I refused to show he got to me.

"Kalnor will see it every day, once I hang it in his workshop."

"He'll never get any work done."

I couldn't help but smile. "Or it might make him work faster, knowing the original is waiting to dine with him."

"True, Your Highness, very true."

No matter how gorgeous Ariv looked in my paintings, it didn't compare to seeing him standing in the shade, glistening with sweat and sand-dust after a hard day's work. I would never leave my gallery if I had him in there with me, looking as he did now.

Ariv leaned over my shoulder, and I caught his scent of sweat, sand, and clove oil. I sat on my hands. It was all I could do not to pull him into my lap.

"I can't wait to see what it looks like with a proper background." And with that, Ariv turned and walked away.

I sighed, staring after him until he disappeared from view. I knew what I wanted. I just wished I knew what *he* wanted.

AFTER SITTING NEXT to the dusty training fields for most of the day, I needed some exercise, and decided to take a stroll through the gardens. I would have liked to go into town to bring Kalnor his painting, but with Neia resting there was no one to accompany me.

The vibrant colours in the southeast corner of the inner gardens always surprised me. The rest of the gardens were more balanced, but this little corner had always been a mix of the wildest colours, with a large blue-leaved roset tree in the middle of it. This was my favourite part of our gardens. So many colours I could use in my paintings, so many different shapes and sizes to play around with.

"Again?"

I stopped. That was Mother's voice. I looked around, but didn't see her near. Maybe she was on the other side of the inner garden wall.

"She'll never stop asking, Héale. She admires his work."

"And we'll refuse every single time."

"Yes. We'll refuse. Your wish is my command, my beautiful Queen."

"Tiaud. Don't jest. We *have* to. You know we do. He can't protect himself."

Me. Mother and Father were talking about me, and someone wanting me to paint for them. I was glad they were on the other side of the wall. I needed to know more, and it would keep them from knowing I was listening in.

"I know, love. He needs someone to watch over him."

"I worry every time he sneaks off. He's so stubborn."

"Stubborn and beautiful like you, Héale."

"He's been so difficult this year. I'm afraid he'll be hurt if we don't keep a better eye on him."

"We can't lock him up, love. Besides, he's been behaving very well this week. Neia's accompanied him every time he went off the castle grounds."

"I know. But what about next week? Next moon?"

"We have to let him go some time, love."

"But not now. And certainly not to Atan to paint Solanta's castle, or her children."

"No, not to Atan."

"If you agree, then why do you insist on these discussions?"

"Because my reasons not to let Llyskel go to Atan are not equal to yours. Solanta is…" Father sighed. "I worry about her, Héale. She was so young when she became queen. Too young. Rass could have been a great help to her, had she not ignored him and insisted on doing it all by herself."

"You know why, Tiaud. We may not agree with their ways, but a royal consort in Atan is nothing like my role in our marriage. Rass has no say, aside from what Solanta grants him. Not the way I do. The way I could have, should I choose."

"Maybe we should talk to Rass."

"*I* will talk to Rass. Solanta wouldn't like her consort talking to you, a king, without her permission."

They were talking about Queen Solanta of Atan and her consort who would be staying with us for a two-day visit to celebrate the harvest negotiations between our countries. It was an annual visit, though not always here. I had never been allowed to join the trips to Atan.

"You talk to Rass. I'll talk to Solanta and will try to convince her to let Llyskel paint Orna during their stay here."

"That's a good idea. Maybe if she wants him to paint Vik as well, he could come for a visit after the harvest season, or when the flowers start blooming again."

I swallowed. They talked so easily about letting Vik come here on his own. Vik was my age, in fact he was younger than me by a moon. Yet they talked about me as if I was incapable of looking after myself. It was not fair.

I clenched my fists and backed away from the wall. I couldn't listen to them any longer. I had to find a way to show them that I *could* take care of myself, that I *could* travel abroad on my own. Well, with one guard, a certain captain maybe, but for company, not protection.

As I walked towards the castle, I couldn't help but imagine Captain Ariv and I, travelling together to visit foreign countries. It was a good thought.

Chapter Three

LYING ON MY bed, naked and aroused, watching Ariv point his shooter at me, I was not completely sure how we got to this point.

I had seen no glimpse of him after he startled me while I was painting Endyrr the day before. Not even when we were all gathered around the fires earlier tonight, ringing in the harvest season and listening to the soldiers telling tales. Yet, the moment I entered my rooms, Captain Ariv appeared right behind me, followed me through the door, and pinned me to the wall as soon as I had put my lamp down.

I smelled alcohol and something sweet on his breath, but his eyes were clear, intent. I shivered, but stayed still. I only had to call out for help to stop him, but I didn't feel threatened, didn't think I was in danger. Not from him.

Though I didn't move, my hands trembled, my heart pounded as though it would burst, and I was certain my cheeks were as red as my hair. I couldn't look away from the intense expression in his eyes. He watched me for a long time, holding me against the wall, frowning, searching. He looked like he wanted to kiss me, but what was he waiting for? Permission to proceed, maybe? Did he really think I would deny him? I nodded with burning cheeks, and only barely kept myself from licking my lips.

The moment he dipped his head and brushed his mouth against mine, I almost stopped breathing. His lips were a little dry, a little cracked, and his tongue a little wet as it darted out, demanding entrance, but warm, so warm.

Someone moaned. It had to be me; his voice was nowhere near as high as that. I itched to touch him, to pull him closer, but his grip on my arms didn't loosen when he teased me or when he slipped his tongue into my mouth. I didn't care how tight his grip was then, as long as he went on kissing me. And when he finally relaxed his grip, I was grateful he was still holding me. Had he not, I would have sagged to the floor.

Capt—no, Ariv. How could I still call him captain, now? Ariv was watching me again, while all I wanted was to be kissed.

"I shouldn't be here."

I froze. He wasn't going to leave me like this, was he?

"I shouldn't, but I can't stay away any longer. Your eyes…" Ariv trailed off. He released my left arm and stroked his thumb along my jaw. "I know what you want, and I can give it to you." With that, he pulled me away from the wall, picked up the lamp, and pushed me up the stairs.

I immediately made for my bed when we reached the top, but he stopped me, grabbing my wrist.

He put the lamp next to my bed. "Show me."

There was no point in pretending I didn't understand him, no point in denying him. I nodded and took him into my gallery. I studied him as he viewed my paintings, the way his eyes went wide as he saw himself in them.

"You have a good memory," he whispered, pointing at the one of him in the forest, stunning the boar. There something of awe in his voice, even as soft as it sounded.

I could only nod.

He pulled me close and kissed me again, hard, demanding, and over before it began. "It's beautiful."

My knees wobbled, but he kept me standing, whispering in my ear to watch the paintings, as he took off my tunic and undid the string on my trousers. He lowered me onto the bench and dropped to his knees to take my boots and trousers off.

"Keep watching."

The heat of his touch shot through me like fire, as he ran his fingers along the inside of my legs and played with my balls. I spread my legs and pushed my hips forward. He stilled my movements with one hand, touched his tongue to my stomach and slowly licked a path upwards. He trailed his hands up my sides as he slithered his tongue across my chest, neck, jaw, lips. And then he kissed me again, dropping his hands to my buttocks, caressing, kneading, and pulling me closer to him until I sat on the edge of the bench. The coarse fabric of his tunic scratched against my belly and my cock. I could feel his against mine through the fabric, hard. He thrust against me, robbing me of my breath more than his kiss did.

Too much, too fast. I didn't want this to end too soon. "Stop," I said into his mouth, or tried, as I was too out of breath to even make a proper sound.

But he did stop, and I immediately regretted telling him to. Ariv stood and undressed himself, slowly, never taking his eyes off me. I couldn't take my eyes off him.

He was tanned all over, and I suddenly longed to paint him practising naked, the sun warming his skin. I didn't even realise I was reaching out until I felt the heat of his skin beneath my fingers. He didn't stop me as I caressed his thigh, watched as I weighed his balls, and shivered as I ran my thumb across the slit of his cock. I rose and pressed my body against his, sighing at the feel of his naked skin against mine. My eyes caught his in the painting, the way they looked down the barrel of his shooter, and I shuddered.

"Yes," he hissed, turning me around, pushing me out of the gallery and onto my bed. "Lie on your back."

I swallowed, but did as I was told. He grabbed something off the floor. My mouth went dry as he showed me his shooter. Oh. He really *did* know what I wanted.

He pointed his shooter at me as he neared the foot of the bed, and I couldn't look away from it. His strong hand, muscles tense around the shooter, the copper glinting in the soft light of the lamp. "Close your mouth, so you won't bite your tongue."

I nodded and closed my mouth, spreading out my arms and legs like a sacrifice from the old tales, and waited. Waited for him to throw a stunning spell at me, waited for the effects to start, waited...

Ariv frowned.

I caught the scent of magic. Was that it? It didn't feel any different.

Ariv looked at his shooter, fiddled with it, shook it, and aimed it back at me. I could clearly see the concentration on his face as he squeezed his fingers around the handle. He frowned again, even before the scent hit me, and pointed the shooter down. The bed shook. He cursed and let the shooter drop to the floor. He formed a bowl with his hands. Pointing them at me, he spoke the spell aloud this time, and practically pushed it at me.

My mouth went dry, but it had nothing to do with arousal or the stunning spell. I shook my head and closed my eyes, clenching my fists by my side to keep from hitting something, someone. This wasn't happening.

The bed dipped, but I kept my eyes closed. I couldn't face Ariv, now. Still, I let him pull me against him, let him stroke my hair, let him mumble words I neither heard nor understood as I lay my head on his shoulder and let him wrap an arm around me.

We lay quiet for a long time as I listened to him breathe, my fists still clenched as I tried to keep myself under control. A feeble control that slipped the moment I felt his lips against my forehead, and I could no longer keep my tears from falling.

I DIDN'T UNDERSTAND what happened. All I knew was that the spell hadn't worked, and three days later, I still couldn't bear to think about it. I tried to put it out of my head, I even locked my gallery and hid away the key, but I still dreamed of it, and it hurt. I kept hoping Ariv would tell me he had done something wrong, had made a mistake, but he was gone by the time I'd woken up, and I hadn't seen him since. I tried to look for him, but with the harvest upon us, the soldiers only trained in the mornings before going down to the fields to help out the farmers.

Now that Queen Solanta and her family had arrived, I wouldn't have time to look for him, anyway. Just as Mother and Father had said in the garden, I was asked to paint a portrait of Orna, Queen Solanta's daughter.

Orna was a quiet little thing with a pretty face. She had dark skin like all the Atan people—sun touched, Father called it —long, light brown hair that hung down in waves, large golden eyes, and plenty of freckles. She made sitting quietly seem effortless, though I had to prompt her to smile every now and then.

I hadn't even told her she had to sit still, but no matter how often I said she was free to move, that I had memorised the pose, Orna stayed in the same position. Still, I had a hard time painting her, and that had nothing to do with her. The composition wasn't a problem, either. I had sat her in front of the orin bushes, hoping the pale green would bring out the warmth of her skin and her smile… when she smiled.

No, the reason I had trouble painting her was because the few paintings that I'd started in the past few days had all gone horribly wrong, had all turned into some depiction of Ariv, and I wasn't even *trying* to paint him. I needed to get him out of my head. I needed to accept that I wasn't going to be seeing him again.

Out of the corner of my eyes, I caught Father talking to Queen Solanta, and the conversation between Mother and Father came back to me. I didn't understand what Father was worried about. Queen Solanta seemed all right to me. She looked a little like Orna from afar, the same long, light brown, wavy hair, sun touched skin, and nose. She probably had freckles, too, when she had been Orna's age. How young had Queen Solanta been when she became queen?

Orna coughed and I looked at her. She was trying hard to sit still, but I could see something was troubling her. She kept twitching her nose.

"You can move for a bit, if you need to," I told her.

Orna immediately started sneezing. I grabbed a cloth and handed it to her.

"Thank you."

That was about the most she had said to me since we started.

She sneezed again, into the cloth this time.

Despite my painting problems, the portrait wasn't going too badly. I'd had better days, but I got her face, with a smile, and I was content with the way her hair turned out. The colour of her dress was where I truly struggled. Not quite grey, not quite blue, but I couldn't seem to get the hue right.

With a sigh, I put a different blue on my palette and

mixed it with the grey I had used before. I held it to the light and shook my head, though it was closer than my earlier attempts. I added more blue of a darker shade, and the result seemed better already.

While Orna settled back into her pose again, the cloth crumpled into one of her hands, I redid part of her dress in the new colour. I nodded. That was much closer to the actual hue, even if it was a rather severe colour for a young girl. When I finally finished the dress, I took a step back.

A high-pitched voice sounded next to me. "Oh, doesn't my princess look pretty?"

I turned to see Queen Solanta standing there, Father close behind her.

I wasn't sure if she meant the painting or Orna herself, but I decided it didn't matter. Orna did look pretty, and her efforts to sit still certainly deserved a compliment. "She does, Your Majesty."

Queen Solanta smiled, but Father frowned. Orna had stopped smiling as well, and once again I found myself wondering why Father was worried about the queen.

AT DINNER, I was seated between Orna and Vik, but neither seemed keen to talk to me. I tried to start a conversation a couple of times, but Orna would only nod and stare at her plate, while Vik looked decidedly bored. I couldn't wait for dinner to end and be allowed to retreat to my rooms.

I had barely seen Vik since he had arrived. He probably spent his afternoon with my brothers. Vik hadn't changed much since the last time they visited. Atan people weren't as broad-built as our people, and Vik was no different. He was tall, dark, and muscular, and his long, black hair easily reached his lower back—black like his father's, Royal Consort Rass. Vik had his mother's and sister's golden eyes, though. Rass' eyes were more a strange mix of green and brown. Not a colour I'd often seen.

With both my companions being quiet, I had plenty of time to glance around the room. Royal Consort Rass sat with Mother, while Father sat next to Queen Solanta. All were talking, though their conversations couldn't be more different. Not that I could hear them, but Father still wore that same frown, while Mother and Royal Consort Rass smiled and laughed as they talked.

The harvest meetings had been held that afternoon, and I hoped Father had managed to arrange for that grain I could never remember the name of, the one that made our bread taste spicy and interesting.

"Mother seems to like your paintings." Vik's voice interrupted my thoughts. I turned towards him, but Vik wasn't looking at me.

"She said she liked the one I did of Orna this afternoon."

"She wants me to sit for a painting tomorrow, before we leave."

Oh, so he wasn't going to be allowed to travel alone. I suppressed a smile at that and scolded myself for feeling so jealous before, especially since Vik didn't seem thrilled about me painting him.

"If you don't want—"

"Mother wants it."

Right. He didn't want to, but he would because his mother wanted it. Painting someone who didn't want to be painted never worked out well. Orna had been quiet, but her face had lit up when she had seen the result. I doubted Vik would enjoy a similar pose. "Will you be training with my brothers tomorrow?"

Vik turned his head. "Yes. And I'm not going to decline

just so you can paint me."

Of course he wasn't. "I can paint you while you're training."

Vik narrowed his eyes and looked at me, through me. His stare was nowhere near as effective as Ariv's had been. When Ariv looked at me like that...

So much for trying to forget about him.

"How?"

"How what?" I asked.

"How would you paint me?"

"However you want. I've painted the soldiers while they're training often enough. Man-to-man, sticks, shooters, swords, whatever you want. You wouldn't even have to hold your pose for long. Once I know how I'm going to paint you, the image will be stuck in my head."

"Is it really that easy for you?"

What could I say to that? *As easy as magic is for you?* No, though I had no doubt he expected it. They knew about me, after all. Mother and Father had never made my deficiency a secret. "Secrets ruin lives," Father once told me. Having it out in the open hadn't made life any easier for me, but I could see his point. I shrugged. "It's what I do."

Vik seemed to think about that, for quite a while, actually. Not until we were leaving the dining room did he speak up again. "All right. Sword. I'd like you to paint me training with my sword."

I hadn't expected anything else. I wasn't sure I could have handled painting him with a shooter, even if theirs looked different from ours. "I'll be at the training field tomorrow, then."

I stopped when I noticed where we were headed. The dance hall. Neither Mother nor Father had said anything about dancing after dinner. Still, they wouldn't appreciate me refusing. Going back to my rooms would have to wait.

Our parents retreated to the back of the dance hall while, in the opposite corner, a harpist, the wife of one of the soldiers, started playing a tune.

Lerran and Riki were the first to dance—they were always the first to dance—quickly followed by Endyrr and Kalnor. Danen, my eldest brother, was not dancing. He sat with our parents, but I didn't see Inau, his wife. Maybe she was checking up on Sirr. I contemplated asking Orna to dance, out of politeness, but Jeon beat me to it, sticking his tongue out at me when Orna couldn't see it. Orna seemed as uncomfortable on the dance floor as she had been at the dinner table, following Jeon along like a wooden puppet. I tried to remember how much younger than me she was. It had to be five years, at least. Only a stripling, a very shy stripling, who was dancing with my dissolute brother, more than a decade her elder.

With a shake of my head, I made for the comfortable window seats, only to be stopped by Vik. He held out a hand.

"Care to dance?"

He would barely talk to me, but he would dance with me? Who would have thought? I couldn't slight a visiting prince, so I took his hand and let him lead me to the dance floor.

Vik was an elegant dancer who knew how to hold a man. Despite my reluctance, it was easy to follow his lead, and we ended up dancing together for quite a while before Jeon wanted his turn.

Strangely enough, once partnered with me, Orna turned out to dance remarkably well for such a shy girl. She liked the faster songs and preferred not to be held while we were dancing, and the more we danced, the more relaxed she seemed. She even managed to smile a few times, though probably because I stumbled during some of the quicker turns.

When we were finally all danced out, Orna and I settled

ourselves in a window seat and enjoyed a cold drink while we watched Jeon and Vik twirl around the room. Jeon was a far better dancer than I was, obviously, but the two of them made dancing look like fighting battle. Neither seemed to want to follow the other or let the other lead.

Endyrr and Kalnor, on the other hand, showed no such strife. They fitted together like they belonged, and glided effortlessly across the floor. As did Lerran and Riki. Perfect examples of how lovers were supposed to dance. I closed my eyes. Would dancing with Ariv be that perfect?

Chapter Four

I DELIVERED A rather sharp blow that hurt my hand more than it did the dummy I was practising on, but I couldn't stop. I *needed* to hit something.

Five days had passed since Ariv sneaked out of my bed. Yet, despite my efforts to put him out of my mind, I found myself training the way he taught me, found myself unable to ignore his instructions. My routine was tighter, my hits more accurate, and I rarely let my left hand drop any more. It made it hard to be angry with him.

I hit the dummy again, with three swift blows. Why had he sneaked out after being so kind to me? He had seen me at my most vulnerable and had stayed and held me until I slept. I couldn't understand why he now seemed to be avoiding me. For five long days. Was it wrong of me to expect this to be more than a one-time affair? Had I read too much in the way he had looked at me? Maybe he had been indulging me, after all: the poor, powerless prince who wouldn't stop crying.

If he came in now, I'd probably scream and rage at him until he left. I might even throw a punch his way if he came close enough. It wouldn't stop me from following his advice. It wouldn't stop me from wanting him, either.

At breakfast, Mother had frowned and sighed as she watched me pick at my bread. A couple of times she had opened her mouth as if to ask a question, only to close it again. The others hadn't seemed to notice her fretting. Father, Danen, and Lerran had been discussing training regimes, with Riki, Lerran's wife and fellow soldier, listening in, while Jeon and Endyrr had been stuffing their faces, as always.

Finally, Mother had scolded me for looking tired and not eating enough, her expression only darkening when I used working out as an excuse. It could hardly tell her what had happened with Ariv. I had held my breath when she turned to Father. One word from him and I'd be done with training, and I needed it, needed to vent. My painting wasn't a useful outlet these days. Every other picture still ended up looking like Ariv in one horrible pose or another, as if he'd been struck down.

When Father had finally looked up, at Mother, at me, studying me with that serious expression of his, he'd shrugged. "Exercise is good for the boy, Héale," was all he said.

Boy. I hadn't been a boy for a good while now. But I would still be allowed to train. That was something, at least. While Mother had held her tongue, her expression told me she didn't agree. She worried too much.

I stepped back from the dummy, looked at the timepiece, and sighed. Still no Ariv. He wasn't going to show up again.

"I always thought you were just fooling around in here, little brother. I didn't know you trained this hard."

I jumped, nearly stumbling over a low bench. Lerran came out of the shadows near the door.

I sighed. "Father sent you?"

Lerran shook his head. "Does he have reason to?"

"Other than Mother hounding him? No, I suppose not." I hoped not.

"Walk with me."

"I need a shower."

"You can shower after."

After what? But I didn't ask Lerran what he meant.

Neia stood outside the hall, ready to follow me. She inclined her head at us when Lerran dismissed her, and made her way towards the castle.

Lerran took me to the far end of the outer gardens, to a secluded area with low benches, surrounded by apple trees and zei fruit bushes. I rarely came here, unless to paint a portrait. I loved using the purple zei fruit and lavender blossoms as a background. And there was something about the combination of sweet apple and tart zei fruit that always made people smile more genuinely.

Lerran told me to sit. I frowned at his formal tone, but did as he asked, even though he stayed on his feet, pacing from one bench to the next.

"Captain Ariv came to me this morning."

I couldn't breathe. Was this why Ariv hadn't approached me?

"His story was a little vague, but he seemed convinced that stunning spells do not work on you. Is that true?"

Oh, no. No, this couldn't be true. He had no right to go to Lerran... I closed my eyes and swallowed. But he had a duty to his king, and Lerran was his commander. It didn't make me feel any better, and I was only lucky he had not gone directly to Father. Was this why Ariv had not come to see me?

"Llyskel. I asked you a question."

I looked up at Lerran, who had a familiar expression in his eyes that I mostly only got from Mother. "Sorry."

"Is it true? About the stunning spell?"

I nodded, then frowned. "I'm not sure. I didn't get stunned, but I'm not sure the spell worked."

"Captain Ariv thought you might say that," Lerran said

with a sigh. "I guess that only leaves one way to check his suspicion."

"No." But my protest was too late. The scent of magic surrounded me as Lerran stunned me...or rather, didn't stun me. I couldn't tell whose eyes went wider when I could still move, his or mine.

"Beloved Okané, it is true. You cannot be stunned."

Somehow, I was less than thrilled about it.

Lerran rubbed his hands together and opened them, pointing them at me.

"What are you doing?"

"I need to make sure it's only stunning that doesn't work."

"What? Are you mad? No, I..." I had no idea what Lerran did, but whatever it was, it seemed to go right through me. I looked behind me just as a zei fruit changed from purple to white. I turned back to Lerran. "You *are* mad. What if you had hit me? How would you have explained that to Father?"

"I've been doing this since I was six, Llyskel. It was a harmless colouring spell that only lasts a couple of hours."

It didn't matter what spell he had thrown at me. No one was allowed to fight with me. My brothers had barely been allowed to play with me, because I was powerless, because I couldn't defend myself. No one had ever dared use magic against me, and now Lerran carelessly threw a spell at me to prove a point? My whole body shook. I tried to push down the anger welling up inside me, tried not to scream, but all I wanted was to punch him, and, fists balled, I advanced on him.

I only realised I had actually hit him when he went down, and I ran.

―∞―

THE LAST THING I needed was Ariv sitting in front of my door, even if the mere sight of him drained my anger. Not that I was going to let him know that. Instead, I crossed my shaking arms in front of my chest and glared at him.

No reaction. I nudged him with my foot, and he shot up, banging his head against my door.

Rubbing his head, Ariv climbed to his feet, and leaned against the door, hefting a heavy looking bag onto his shoulder. "I'm sorry."

I blinked, wondering whether he was apologising for falling asleep or for telling Lerran about the spell. "He threw magic at me!"

Ariv flinched, and I nearly caved. I wanted to let him know I understood why he told Lerran, even if I didn't like it, but I had no intention of telling him I wasn't angry at him. He wasn't getting away that easily.

He pushed away from the door, pulled me to him by my shoulders and wrapped his arms around me. "You're shaking. If he hurt you…"

"His stunning spell did nothing to me," I told Ariv. Just like his hadn't done anything, no matter how I tried to tell myself he had misfired. "The other one…" I shuddered.

"What?"

"It was as if it went right through me. Like I wasn't even standing there. A zei fruit in the bush behind me changed colour, but it didn't work on me."

Ariv froze for a moment, but then he started shaking. I thought it was from anger, at first, until he snorted and burst out laughing. I tried to step away from him, but he wouldn't let me go. He kept holding me, and kept laughing.

"Sorry," he said, in between the laughter. "He used a colouring spell?"

I didn't understand what was so funny about that, but

Ariv was still laughing. When he finally stopped, he took a couple of breaths and changed his hold on me so he could look me in the eye. "That is probably the first spell every six-year-old learns, not to mention the least harmful."

"That's what he..." Oh. "Lerran was trying to be careful."

Ariv grinned at me, almost touching his forehead to mine. "He was, but I'm glad you didn't change colour."

I swallowed, guilt about striking my brother welling up inside me. I shouldn't have, even if his actions had made me angry. One account of a botched spell and he thought he could do what he liked. He should have explained, should have... I sighed.

"Tell me."

"I struck Lerran."

Ariv's grin never wavered. "Good for you."

"What?"

"It was about time he found out how strong you really are. I hope you floored him."

I remembered seeing Lerran lying on the ground and nodded, not sure I should be happy about it.

"Good. Now, invite me in, so I can show you what I brought you. I think you're going to like this."

He let me go and I opened my door, but I didn't let him in right away. I turned towards him. "Five days, Ariv."

"I had to get my head around some things."

"About telling Lerran."

"About you and me. About getting you what you want. But, yes, about telling Commander Lerran as well."

I doubted he could get me what I wanted if spells didn't work on me, but I couldn't punish him for making an effort, could I? I stepped aside and let him in.

He yawned and stretched, until he caught me looking. "Harvesting season is more strenuous than practice, and I haven't been sleeping well. After our conversation this morning, Commander Lerran granted me the rest of the day off."

"And you came here for a nap?"

Ariv raised an eyebrow, before shaking his head and beaming at me. "Believe me, the last thing I want to do when I'm around you is nap."

I couldn't help but shiver at that. "You mentioned presents?"

"Upstairs."

STANDING NAKED IN front of my bed, my calves flush against the edge, I pulled on my hands, which were held tightly against my body by ropes tied in an intricate pattern of knots. I looked down at Ariv binding my legs, my ankles.

"Stop squirming or you'll fall."

I straightened, took a deep breath, and forced myself to be still, which was impossible with the way I was trembling. When Ariv had started binding my upper arms, I thought it would be easy enough. It was only a bit of rope, right?

Wrong. With every tremble the rope tightened and moved. It made me feel...unsettled. Unsettled, and light-headed, and a little out of breath. I had no idea what Ariv would do next, even while I was still able to watch him wrap and twist and knot the rope. But he wasn't merely paying attention to the rope. He touched my skin with every pass, traced his fingers over my body next to the rope, teasing me, torturing me. He kept telling me how gorgeous I looked, but I couldn't believe him. It was just me wrapped in rope. Nothing special. Not until I found myself aroused, as much by his touch as by the way the rope rubbed my skin, could I believe him. I wished I had a mirror, wished he had left one of my hands free so I could paint myself through his eyes.

Ariv rose to his feet, as naked and hard as I was, with an expression in his eyes that told me how much he enjoyed putting me in this situation. He said he had done this before, said his partners had always been thoroughly satisfied, and I had no choice but to believe him now.

But no matter how confident Ariv seemed that this would help me get what I wanted, I couldn't imagine this coming even close. I liked the feeling, I wouldn't deny that, not to myself and not to him, but I couldn't see it working.

Tracing the patterns on my chest, Ariv stepped closer, put a hand behind my neck and bent down. The kiss was soft, warm, and far too short. I opened my mouth to protest when he stepped back again, but froze as he pushed me.

My breath hitched and my heart pounded as I fell, my instincts telling me to move my arms, to catch my fall, but, bound as I was, I couldn't. I cursed Ariv's lineage, even as I landed on my bed, softer than I expected. I hiccupped and lay there, catching my breath.

Ariv rested his hand on my chest and grinned.

I glared at him and thought how fortunate it was for him that I couldn't wipe that stupid grin off his face.

"You were perfectly safe."

I sighed, hating that he was right. I knew the bed was behind me. It wasn't his fault I forgot as I was falling. He didn't have to look so smug about it, though.

"All right, now?"

I nodded and kept my mouth shut. Being bound the way I was, it probably wasn't wise to keep cursing him.

"Good. Now, stay here while I prepare the next part."

He moved out of view before I could react. What did he mean, the next part? This wasn't enough?

Waiting for Ariv to return was hard, as hard as lying still would be if I hadn't been bound. My muscles twitched, and I couldn't stop myself from trying to move my fingers, my hands, causing the ropes to scratch across my chest, my wrists. I gasped at the unexpectedly pleasant sensations and stared at the ceiling, hoping he wouldn't leave me like this for too long. I wanted him to touch me.

Still, as tight as he had bound me, it didn't feel uncomfortable, even though I could clearly feel the rope, the knots. I couldn't help but wonder what he was doing in my gallery, couldn't help thinking about how often he had done this and to whom. But before I could even think of becoming jealous, my gallery door opened with a bang.

I looked up, only to find myself staring at a shooter. My breath hitched, and I spread my arms, tried to spread my arms, but, of course, they wouldn't budge. Beyond the shooter, Ariv stood dressed in his trousers, his expression serious and focussed as he raised his shooter. His shooter. The sunlight coming through the window lit up the copper hue, not as much as it did outside, but it was bright nonetheless. I swallowed and tried to take deep breaths as I waited. I watched Ariv's fingers clench around the handle on the trigger, the muscles of his hand twitching, tensing up. I couldn't look away as he aimed the shooter at me, couldn't look away as the familiar scent of magic reached my nose.

My whole body tensed up, and I clenched my hands as the ropes dug into my flesh and restricted my movements even more. Ariv lowered his shooter, tracing it up my leg, slowly, and still I watched him, my heart pounding, my breath coming in short gasps. I wiggled my hands, itching to touch my cock, itching for him to touch it, and still I couldn't look away from the way he traced his shooter across my stomach and up my chest.

"You feel it now, don't you?" He trailed the shooter past my shoulder and down my right arm.

"Please." There was nothing else I could say. I so wanted him to keep touching me, to fuck me.

He moved the shooter close to my cock, and I moaned. If he did that again, I would come. I closed my eyes and clenched my fists even tighter.

The next moment, the shooter lay on my chest, and when I opened my eyes, Ariv knelt across my hips, naked. "What?" How had he managed to get his trousers off this fast?

"Shh." He looked into my eyes, grabbing my cock in his hand, guiding it.

I cried out as he lowered himself onto me, felt my cock sink into the warmth of his body. Overcome with sensation, I couldn't think, couldn't process. I could only feel, and it felt so good. My muscles screamed as I tried to push my hips up. Even as little as that caused the ropes to dig into my flesh, to rub, scratch, and set my body on fire. I couldn't look away as Ariv fucked himself on my cock, up and down and up and down, biting his lip, moaning and gasping. I soared higher and higher until something deep inside of me exploded, and I came with a shout. Ariv grunted as my head sank back onto the bed, and his come splattered my chest.

I lay there, panting, trembling, body weak as jelly, with Ariv leaning heavily on top of me, breathing puffs of air into my face. Despite begging him not leave me, Ariv rose and loosened the ropes faster than I thought possible, before rubbing my chest with a damp cloth and climbing in next to me.

More satisfied and relaxed than I had ever been, I snuggled closer into Ariv's embrace. "You were right." I grinned at how scratchy and hoarse my voice sounded.

"I was." It wasn't a question.

"You promised me and it was…" I raised my head to look

at him. "It was everything I imagined."

"Even if I didn't fuck you like you asked?"

"Yes." I played with the curls on his chest. As tempted as I was to ask him about it, I didn't want him to think I hadn't enjoyed myself. "I was surprised."

"You were gorgeous. All tied up in my knots, wide-eyed, and writhing and sweating as I rode you."

He had the same look in his eyes as when he had been tying me up, and that was all the explanation I needed. He liked it that way. I liked it that way. What more was left to say? I kissed him, felt him open up for me, and shivered in his arms as I deepened the kiss.

Chapter Five

BREAKFAST WAS ALREADY served when I entered the private dining room. I was late, but as I greeted my family, I noticed that Lerran's chair was still empty as well. I gave Mother a quick hug before sitting down next to Endyrr.

"Late night, little brother?"

I nodded as I traced my right thumb across my left wrist, only barely suppressing a shudder.

"Do—"

The door slammed open and Lerran stumbled in, sweating as if he had been running, and sporting a rather ugly looking black eye. I winced as he paused next to my seat, grinning.

"Good morning, little brother. The flowers in the garden are particularly vibrant today, are they not?"

I had no clue what to say to that. I hadn't even looked out of my window this morning. I had been too busy gazing at Ariv as he dressed. Lerran moved on and greeted our parents as jovially as always, while I was still waiting for a comment, a jibe at yesterday's altercation. None came. Instead it seemed business as usual. Lerran sat next to Danen and immediately started chatting about training schedules for the morning, though I did notice he and Father exchanging glances.

Aside from the work discussions and the occasional question from Mother—to me about what I planned to paint, and to Danen about Inau's increasing tiredness and Sirr's volatile moods—breakfast was rather quiet. I found myself touching my wrists every chance I got, though I didn't dare look at them. I couldn't stop myself. Knowing the rope marks were still visible—faint, but visible—touching them, just rubbing my thumb across them, made me shudder and remember. At times I had to fight not to close my eyes and forget where I was. It was as if I'd never had sex before. I smiled at myself. Not like this, I hadn't. Not this satisfying.

Being so wrapped up in my own little world, I almost missed someone entering the room. Had not my entire family fallen quiet, I wouldn't have noticed. I turned my head towards the door and froze. Ariv stood in the doorway, dressed in full captain's garb, carrying a small wicker basket.

"Good morning, Your Majesty," Ariv said as he bowed towards Father, before turning to Mother. "Your Majesty, Highnesses. I hope I'm not disturbing your meal."

"Not at all, Captain," Father answered him. "Enter and state your business."

Ariv bowed again and walked towards me, slowly, looking straight at me with a serious expression on his face. I didn't know whether to shiver or swallow, and I ended up gripping the sides of my seat as I tried to keep breathing.

"Your Highness," Ariv said as he reached out with one hand.

I grabbed it, and Ariv pulled me up so we stood face to face.

He held out the basket as he spoke the traditional request to court me. "Llyskel. Our paths have crossed and twined. You complete mine. I hope you will let me complete yours."

In the basket lay a single kozal bud on a leafless stem. It was rather backwards for Ariv to ask permission to court me *after* we had sex, but, from what I'd seen of him over the years, it didn't surprise me that he was a traditional man, sexual appetite aside.

I took the basket without a word. Taking the basket was to show my consent, my willingness to consider his offer. My answer to Ariv would have to be returned in the same traditional way: a return gift of a flower to express my own intentions. After what he'd done for me, I had no desire to let him go, and I couldn't wait to see what he would come up with for our first public outing as a couple.

As Ariv disappeared through the door, I sat, holding the basket in my lap, and looked at the beautiful bud. I tried not to wonder whether he would have asked if his rope trick hadn't worked. Hidden by the basket, I lifted my sleeve and smiled at the faint rope marks around my wrists.

Jeon whistled. "Quite the catch, brother. However did you manage to snag *him?*"

I shook my head as the others joined in and silently suffered their teasing. Lerran, though, did not say a word. He merely winked at me.

"Boys, leave Llyskel be and finish your meals," Mother admonished my brothers as she passed the raisin bread to Father.

She smiled and reached around Endyrr to squeeze my shoulder as I set the basket next to my plate and grabbed my spoon to finish my forgotten bowl of soup.

"Llyskel."

I turned to face Father.

"See me in my chambers after breakfast."

—∞—

FATHER'S COMMAND STILL echoed through my head as I walked the corridor leading to his chambers. I wasn't surprised by his summons. I had no doubt Lerran had talked to him about the results of his little test. Not to mention me hitting him. I reached Father's chambers and knocked on the door. No point in postponing the inevitable.

"Come in."

Taking a deep breath, I opened the door and entered. I waited until he motioned me to sit before taking the rigid high-backed chair in front of his desk, folding my hands in my lap.

Father sat back, his blue eyes inscrutable as he studied me. I never knew what he thought. I used to think it was because he was the king. Now I knew he had always been this difficult to read.

"It's been brought to my attention that we underestimated you."

Finally.

"Lerran said your aim was good, but your follow-through left something to be desired. I think it's time you started training with a proper partner, instead of fooling around with those dummies."

I gaped at him, but he had not finished yet.

"Even though Lerran suggested Captain Ariv, I was more than surprised when the captain came to see me early this morning to inform me of his relationship with you and ask my permission to court you. I thought I was meeting him to discuss your training."

Ariv had gone to Father? But surely he knew I reached maturity months ago. I thought of the kozal bud and smiled. Ariv didn't do things halfway, did he?

"Llyskel. Pay attention when I talk to you."

I looked at Father. "I'm sorry. It's... I expected to be scolded for attacking Lerran."

"Should you attack any of your brothers in future, there certainly will be punishment," Father said. "However, seeing as Lerran provoked you by using spells on you, I'll let it go. That leaves the matter of your training. Do you feel comfortable with Captain Ariv training you, considering your relationship?"

"Yes. Yes, of course." I could barely suppress a shiver as I imagined him standing behind me, holding my wrists to adjust my stance. The wrists still bearing faint rope marks.

"Good. Which brings me to my next point." He studied me again. "I hear spells don't seem to work on you."

I blinked, clearing my thoughts. "The stunning spell didn't work on me, no, nor did Lerran's colouring spell."

Father nodded, mouth drawn in a straight line as he rubbed his beard. "Inau says that Sirr loves painting with you."

What did that have to do with spells not working on me? "She does. She often joins me when I'm painting outside."

"And you don't mind? You don't like having Neia around."

"I don't like the *reason* Neia hangs around. I don't need protection, Father."

"So I'm starting to learn."

Was he really? I sighed in relief.

"I'm not dismissing Neia of her duties completely, Llyskel. However, I don't see why you can't move around on your own within the castle walls."

Maybe I should have punched Lerran years ago, if this was the result.

Father rose. "Follow me."

I frowned. "Where are we going?"

"Training hall. You need to be tested."

"Tested?"

"For this so-called immunity against magic."

I hoped he was jesting, but the moment we entered the

training hall it became obvious he wasn't. He was serious and thorough, a bit too serious and thorough. For the rest of the morning he threw spell after spell at me until he was close to tapping into his reserves. None of the spells affected me, however. Some I could feel going through me, like the colouring spell, while others seemed to just not work, like the stunning spell. I couldn't say the same of the poor dummies, which were in pieces by the time Father finally decided he'd had enough.

Heaving and leaning heavily against one of the beams, he grimaced at me. "Inau will be grateful to get some rest while you watch Sirr."

That was as much of a compliment as I would get from him right now.

At least I thought so, until he added, "Your training with Captain Ariv starts tomorrow. Your lack of power prevents me from enlisting you. Though I hope you will never see a war in your lifetime, you will at least be prepared for it."

He looked surprised as I threw myself at him, but didn't hesitate to wrap his arms around me. "Thank you," I whispered.

"You're welcome, son. Now, go save Inau from that volatile grandchild of mine. She needs her rest and I have a harvest to oversee. I'm late enough as it is."

Despite his dismissal, we left the training hall together, walking up to the castle side by side in silence, the way I had seen him walk with my brothers after training, the sun warming our faces. For the first time since I'd found out I would never be like them, I felt like I belonged here.

"If you accept him, I have no doubt Captain Ariv will make you a fine husband, Llyskel. Invite him to dinner soon, so you don't worry your mother," Father said as he turned towards the stables, as if he had no doubt I would accept Ariv's request. "Don't tell her about the training. Danen is nowhere near ready to be king."

—∞—

SIRR'S TONGUE STUCK out of her mouth as she drew whiskers on the cat she was painting. It looked more like a large blob with dark eyes, but it was a change from the trees and stars she normally painted. She didn't look up as I mixed some red and yellow to get the hue of her dress right. I doubted she even noticed I was painting her. She had been rather quiet since we started painting, but Inau had warned me she didn't talk much these days, aside from her tantrums. I didn't mind. It gave me time to focus on my work, this being the first painting I had done in days, and it gave me time to think.

Father's words were on my mind as I thought of the kozal bud lying on my desk and, once again, I pondered my place here. No matter how often they had told me I belonged, I had never truly felt it. I never lacked for anything—quite the opposite, I had been overprotected, coddled—and still I often felt like an outsider.

I couldn't blame it all on my family, either. I could have challenged them, could have demanded, could have thrown a tantrum that might have even put Sirr to shame. I should have, but I never had. I let them treat me the way they did, resigned myself to my position the way they had, as though it was set in stone that powerless meant weak. As much as I kept convincing myself I wasn't weak, I had never tried to prove them wrong.

Now that I *had* proved them wrong, it was time I proved to myself I *did* belong.

"How's this look, Uncle?" Sirr held her dripping brush away from her painting.

I quickly grabbed the brush and put it in the water bowl. Though, at first glance, her picture looked like a blob with a tail that ran off the paper, the detail she had put into the whiskers and eyes was amazing for a six-year-old.

Sirr grinned as I told her she had done a good job, and her grin turned even brighter when I helped her make the cat's fur more lifelike. Soon she was busy cross-hatching, tongue firmly sticking out of her mouth again. She still hadn't noticed I was painting her.

When I finished, I turned around, but Neia was nowhere to be seen. She had probably been sent to join her group in helping with the harvest. Neia was more at home as a soldier than having to follow me everywhere. Still, it was strange not having her around.

Sirr was still cross-hatching cat fur, but I didn't want to start a new painting. I stood and stretched my legs a bit, walking around the garden—separated from the grounds by a hedge of orin bushes—and making sure to keep an eye on Sirr.

I could barely believe I would officially start training with Ariv tomorrow. Though I'd assured Father it was comfortable with the idea, I wasn't so certain now. His presence had already been a distraction *before* we'd had sex. Still, Riki and Lerran seemed to have no trouble being so close to each other every day, and I wasn't going to refuse a chance to see more of Ariv. This being harvest season, I had to grab every opportunity.

Between meeting Father and spending time with Sirr, I hadn't had time to go out into the south garden and cut a sprig of dark green leaves from the venoli tree. I would have to do that as soon as Inau had rested and relieved me of babysitting duty, so I could present it to Ariv tonight.

Though there were more ways of answering a request to court, there was only one possible answer for me. No blue roset leaf, like Riki gave Lerran, meaning she would not be opposed to including a third in their relationship, and certainly no lavender zei blossom that would indicate an open relationship. No, a sprig of the venoli tree was what Ariv would receive from me. I didn't share, and I hoped Ariv didn't either.

I would have rather presented the sprig after our training, but we would be alone then, and that was not how it was supposed to be done. It had to be done in public, and if Ariv could face my family at breakfast, I could face his tired soldiers after a day of harvesting, no matter how uncomfortable that made me feel.

Which meant waiting at the gate for Ariv to return from the harvest.

I was wrong. This was nothing like Ariv facing my family at breakfast. I stood by the gate, venoli sprig carefully hidden in my sleeves, as the soldiers returned from the harvest. They all looked at me as they passed, no doubt wondering what his Highness was doing out here this late.

Endyrr was the first of my brothers to pass me. He nodded at his group and approached me. "Waiting for your captain?"

I nodded. Of course Endyrr knew exactly why I was here.

"I think his group is the last to arrive. They were still loading their last cart when we left." Endyrr rested his hand on my shoulder. "Good luck, little brother."

"Thank you."

Endyrr sprinted back to his group. I watched him as I tried hard to ignore the stares from the soldiers passing by.

Danen, Riki, and Jeon walked by together, deep in conversation. They barely even noticed me, which was a relief, because Jeon would no doubt have laughed at me. He didn't care much for the traditional courting rituals and was always quick to make a joke of them. They didn't fit his view on relationships, not with the casual way he dated his lovers, male and female. Still, I had a feeling that someday someone would offer Jeon a lavender zei blossom, and Jeon would accept. I was certain he would. He just wasn't ready yet.

I winced when Lerran passed a few moments later. His eye was still nearly black, though surrounded by hues of purple, green, and yellow. Lerran smiled and winked as he passed, before saying something to the soldiers next to him. They laughed. Had he told them how he got his black eye?

It couldn't be long now before Ariv would arrive; Lerran was Ariv's commander, after all.

When I finally did spot Ariv, he looked as worn out as the rest of the soldiers, ready for nothing but a shower and bed. He chatted to a soldier next to him, facing away from me. For a moment, I thought about going back to the castle before he noticed me. What had I been thinking? They had just finished a hard day of work and here I was, waiting for him to postpone his rest.

But before I could slip away, Ariv faced me, his tired eyes trained on mine, his lips curling into a grin. No turning back, now.

I waited until they reached the gate before approaching him, venoli sprig still hidden within my sleeves. Ariv paused, motioning his group to do the same. I swallowed as they all turned towards me, watched me, but I didn't stop. I kept walking until I stood in front of Ariv.

"Captain Ariv." Pushing back my sleeves, I revealed the venoli sprig and held it up to him. "Ariv. Our paths have crossed and twined. I would gladly merge my path with yours."

Ariv's wide grin, despite his obvious tiredness, made waiting worth it. He took the spring and studied it in the shimmering light, before pocketing it in his trousers.

I expected him to nod at me and take his group home, but Ariv, traditional as he turned out to be, did no such thing. He stepped forward, pulled me to him, and kissed me in front of his group. I froze. I didn't feel comfortable with everyone watching us share such a private moment, but feeling his lips against mine, dry and rough from being out in the fields all day, made me forget all about them.

Ariv trembled against me, leaning hard on me when we ended the kiss, his forehead against mine. "Good night," he whispered.

"Good night, Ariv." It was hard not to try and persuade him to come to my rooms, but he needed his sleep, and I had to let him go.

I couldn't wait for the harvest to be over.

Chapter Six

WHEN I ARRIVED in the training hall, I half expected Ariv to be all business about training me. Instead he grinned and kissed me, wearing the venoli sprig pinned on his tunic, a clear sign he accepted my terms.

I didn't want to let go of him, but after another kiss, and another, and another, Ariv pulled away and shook his head. "Time to work," he said. My mind was slow to catch up, but Ariv handed me a cup of sweet tea and told me to drink it.

It may have been sweet, but it was no tea I'd ever had before. "What's in this?"

"Maris root. Helps to wake you up."

"But I am awake," I protested.

Ariv raised his eyebrow. I sighed and focussed on what he wanted me to do.

He had me do laps first, warming up, practising my stance for the longest time, before he finally told me to face him, fight him. I remembered flooring Lerran and wasn't exactly eager to start, but Ariv, at least, expected my punches and blocked them at the right time. When he suddenly didn't, I felt his head fling backwards as I hit his jaw. I froze and stepped back.

He stopped me by grabbing my wrist. "Llyskel. Look at me. I don't bruise easily. I may not have expected quite that much force, but I wouldn't have let you fight me if I didn't think I could handle it, that *you* could handle it."

He didn't bruise easily, he said. I thought about all those times I had seen him fight, seen him throw his soldiers to the floor, seen him fall. He was one of the strongest soldiers in the field. He was right; he could handle this, and I needed to handle it or training me was a waste of his time. I shook my head. All these years, I wanted to be trained like my brothers, and here I was, losing my nerve. "I've never hit anyone, before Lerran."

Ariv nodded. "We're going to work on that." He put his hands back in position again and grinned. "Wait until I get you to train with the short blades. You are going to love those."

My eyes must have popped out, because he started laughing. "Don't worry, Your Highness. We'll start small. Are you ready to have another go?"

I glared at him, but nodded nonetheless. Did he have to use my title to mock me?

I checked my stance, checked my arms, and started dancing around him again. Ariv's blocking changed. Some of my punches almost made it past his defences, others Ariv stopped as soon as I struck out. And he wouldn't shut up. He kept commenting, kept telling me what to do, what not to do, making it hard to stick to the rhythm I had been practising. Even harder because he kept changing rhythm on me, forcing me to change mine, again and again, until I could barely remember a rhythm at all.

By the time he finally decided I'd had enough, my tunic was drenched in sweat and I had trouble catching my breath, but I felt so good. I'd managed to hit him twice more. Or rather, he had *let* me hit him twice more, even if neither of the punches were as hard as that first one.

"We need to work on the way you reveal your punches. It's too easy to tell what you're going to do." Ariv wiped his face and hands with his tunic. "Your face is too open."

I swallowed as he stepped up to me, eyes boring into mine. This close, I could see their rich, dark brown colour, I could even see the tiny scattered specks of gold in them. He raised a hand to my cheek, moving even closer.

"Like a book, so open. I see all of you," he said, right before he brushed his lips to mine.

A mere hint of moist lips against mine, over before my brain even registered it. I closed my eyes and leaned forward, snaking my hand behind his head with no intention of letting him go. Ariv refused to give me what I wanted and kept his lips together. He put his hands on my chest and stepped back.

I opened my eyes and reached out.

Ariv grabbed my hand and brushed his lips across it. "You barely have time for a shower before the company starts flooding in. Somehow I doubt you're ready to have them catch us trousers down and my tongue down your throat."

He had a point. I sighed.

Ariv grabbed his shooter from the rack and walked away from me, "I'll make it up to you."

I couldn't help glance at my wrists. The memory alone was enough to make me shiver in anticipation.

Ariv stopped in the doorway and faced me, shooter hanging loosely from his hand, and I suddenly itched to paint him like this, with the morning sun creating a halo of light around his shaded profile. The muscles in his shoulders caught the light beautifully, making them seem more pronounced. I imagined kissing him there, at the point where his shoulders met his neck, and all thoughts of painting him disappeared. He was strong and gorgeous, and I wanted him.

"Meet me at the gate at the dinner bell."

I blinked, and he was gone.

FOR EVERYONE BUT me, watching Sirr was as dangerous today as it had been uneventful yesterday. No soldier had even dared using the entrance in the wall opposite the garden. They'd all had to use the one on the other side of the training hall because Sirr had been firing off magic left and right all day.

Of course, Sirr had no idea she was doing it, and spent her play time giggling as she chased a hapless butterfly around the garden with a large net. That was fine with me, because while she was running around, I was making a game of avoiding being hit by her erratic magic. I didn't need to avoid the magic, but it was fun to try. It started out as a game to test my responses, to see if I could be quick enough, but it turned into a lesson in magical theory—lessons that had been deemed unimportant due to my lack of power.

Until today, I had always thought magic preceded its scent, not the other way around. It took me a while to catch on to it, to how I sensed the magic whoosh over me *after* I'd already ducked, and *after* I'd smelled its scent, mostly because it didn't seem possible for me to out-duck an aimed spell, let alone an unintentional one. But the more I played, the more I started paying attention not just to the smells but also to the actual spells as they passed me, passed through me even. That was when I finally caught on to the order.

I wondered why I hadn't noticed when Father had been testing me, though I vaguely remembered the training hall being filled with the scent of magic. Also, I hadn't felt all the spells Father had thrown at me, while I could feel all of Sirr's magic, since she wasn't actually casting formed spells.

According to Inau, whenever Sirr burned energy, it

would come out in little bursts containing raw magic. On days like this, when the bursts of magic didn't seem to let up, Sirr would be exhausted before lunch and sleep the rest of the day to replenish. I could already see she was becoming tired. Her jumps weren't as high as they had been earlier, and she didn't giggle as much as pant.

Sirr's volatility would end when she became aware of what she was doing. No one could tell her that: she needed to feel it for herself. Obviously, she hadn't yet.

I had no doubt all this was common knowledge, but I wished someone had taught me when I was younger. It felt strange, only now learning about the magic that was so ingrained into our history, our daily lives, at the hand of a volatile six-year-old.

Just as Sirr paused and turned to me, I caught the scent of another burst. I ducked and rolled out of the way of the magic flowing past me.

"Why are you rolling in the grass like that, Uncle Llyskel?"

I rose. "Because you're throwing magic at me."

Sirr stopped and pouted. "Mummy says I can't help it."

"I know."

"Am I hurting you like I hurt Bess?" Bess was one of the kitchen maids.

I shook my head. "No, Sirr. That's why Grandfather asked me to play with you. You can't hurt me. Didn't Mummy tell you?"

Sirr frowned and bit her lip. "She said you have a good shield."

That was what Sirr had been told. It bothered me, because no adult was going to believe that story. Everyone knew I didn't possess any magic. I wanted everyone to know about my immunity, too. I wanted everyone to know I wasn't weak, but Father forbade it. "To protect you," he had said. "Yes, because I have a good shield."

Her head tilted, Sirr looked at me. "But why are you ducking?"

"I'm playing a game."

That seemed to cheer her up. "Can I play too?"

"You are. I'm trying not to be hit by your magic."

"But you have a shield. You don't have to duck."

Suddenly, the roles were reversed, and I was teaching my six-year-old niece about magic. The little I knew, that was.

NEIA DIDN'T SEEM completely comfortable as she posed for me at the edge of the fen with the waterfall roaring behind her, despite her enthusiasm when I told her I was going to paint on our way here. She stood still, her hands clasped behind her back, half looking at the fen, half looking at me, her thick, dark blond hair hanging loose around her face. Because she wore her uniform, I intended to paint only her face, but Neia had insisted I do a full body portrait. She was proud to be a soldier. Undoing her braid had been her only concession.

A soldier at rest, if barely. If only she would show more of a smile, or would relax into her stance. But despite my attempts to lighten her seriousness, Neia's body seemed poised to jump into action at any time, and she kept turning her head at every movement around us. "To watch for intruders," she'd said when I asked her to hold still. Even posing, Neia was doing her job.

"I saw your painting of the water nymphs," Neia said as she looked across the fen again. "Do you think they'll show themselves today?"

"They don't come out often. Besides, it's too early for

them."

"Pity. I'd have loved to see them."

"If we stay here long enough, we might." I doubted it—in all the times I'd been here they'd rarely shown themselves to me —but I liked the look of hopeful longing it created on Neia's face. A look I had to paint, because it fitted her so much better than a smile.

Surrounded by the sound of the thundering waterfall, I finished my painting of Neia. Her expression gave the painting a melancholy feel, her head turned away as if she was looking at something just out of frame, her dark blond hair nicely framed by the blues and whites of the waterfall. I hoped she would like it.

Neia's head snapped to the left, her eyes narrowing as she studied something behind me. I turned when her eyes widened and she reached for her shooter, and froze when I smelled magic. Behind me, Neia gasped. I couldn't look away from the shooters pointed at us, but I let out a breath in relief when I heard a thump instead of a splash; at least Neia hadn't fallen into the fen.

The shooters looked different from ours—some dull grey material I didn't recognise instead of copper, and the hands holding them dark like those of the Atan people—but the effect on me was the same. I stood frozen, eyes drawn to the shooters, and swallowed against the arousal I couldn't suppress. I should have ducked, run, jumped into the water, should have done something, but all three shooters were pointed at me, and I couldn't move, couldn't look away. Even if I could move, now, it would be too late. I couldn't risk letting them know their magic didn't work on me. Who knew what they'd do if they found out?

In that moment, I was convinced Mother had always been right. I couldn't protect myself. Despite being immune to magic, despite my training, a shooter pointed at me was all it took to render me useless.

I'm sorry.

The zing of a shooter pierced through the sounds of the thundering waterfall. When the scent of magic reached me, I counted to five and let myself drop back as if hit, hoping the moss would cushion my fall.

I'm sorry.

My head hit a rock before bouncing on the moss. I nearly bit my tongue at the pain, but I didn't cry out and didn't move. Closing my eyes, I hoped they believed my act.

I was grabbed and carried through the forest. The movement made my stomach lurch. I tried to remember where we were going, but they weren't taking paths I recognised. Sometimes leaves brushed my face, sometimes they tilted me sideways to worm their way through the dense trees. All I was aware of was the sound of the waterfall fading into the background.

I'm sorry, Ariv.

It was silly to think of our outing, of not being at the gate when he expected me. I wanted to scream, but I couldn't give myself away and my head was pounding. So I stayed silent and let them carry me farther and farther away from my home.

Finally, I was hoisted into some sort of cart.

"Should we bind him, Overseer?"

"No. No marks."

"What if—"

"Then we'll stun him again. Understood?"

"Yes, Overseer."

Overseer? What sort of rank was that? There was no such rank in Father's army. Maybe they were slave traders. It had been a long time since those had ventured into Eizyrr, and I only knew about them from rumours, but it was all I could

think of. They might not even know who I am; they could have
stumbled across us by accident, just a painter and his model. Of
course, with Neia dressed in soldier's garb, I knew I was only
deceiving myself.

Neia. Had they taken her, too, or had they left her at the
waterfall? Would they have let her live? I tried to convince
myself she was alive and would alert Father, my family, and
Ariv about my abduction. They would come for me. Ariv would
come for me.

For now, though, I was on my own, and I needed to
know where they were taking me. So, I swallowed against the
pain and the nausea, and listened for their voices, hoping they
would give me a clue about who they were and who they
worked for. I listened to the sounds around me, the rustling of
the leaves, birds, boars, a wolf even, hoping to pick up
something that would tell me where I was or where we were
going.

It became colder, more windy, and I realised we had
reached the far edge of the forest. We were nowhere near the
castle. The ground under the cart was uneven and the footfalls
sounded soft, as though my captors were walking on grass or
moss, which meant open fields, not farm land.

And the only open fields on this side of the forest were
the ones separating Eizyrr from Atan. They were taking me to
Atan.

Chapter Seven

MY HEAD HURT. It was throbbing, following the rhythm of my heartbeat, and I wished it would stop. I couldn't think. There was something in the back of my mind, something I should be doing, had been doing. What was it?

Ariv. I was meeting Ariv at the gate. Had the dinner bell sounded already?

I carefully rolled onto my back, wriggling until I lay comfortably on the soft bedding. Why did my head hurt so much?

I opened my eyes. The image was a bit fuzzy, but of one thing I was certain. This was not my bedroom. I closed my eyes again. Where was I?

Too many questions I had no answers to. I needed someone to answer, but just as I wanted to call out, I remembered I had been at the waterfall, painting Neia, and I remembered falling. I faked falling because people were pointing shooters at me. Then they carried me through the forest, towards Atan.

Yes, Atan, that was where they had taken me. But why?

Opening my eyes again, I blinked a couple of times to clear the image. The room was dark, a reddish brown hue on both walls and ceiling. I turned my head to look around and instantly regretted it. My head burst with pain, and the throbbing got worse. Just my luck to hit a rock instead of landing on the moss as I had intended. I breathed against the pain until it became more bearable, and tried to study the room without moving my head. There were large, darkened windows. It seemed to be twilight outside. How long had I been here? And where was Neia? I hoped she was all right. I wished I knew whether they'd brought her or left her behind.

I hoped they'd brought her. I could use some help getting out of here.

I lifted my hands, relieved they weren't bound. "No marks," I remembered the overseer saying. If only my head didn't burst at even the slightest movement, I could have planned my escape already. But all I could do now was close my eyes, and hope I'd feel well enough to try later.

My thoughts of *later* vanished when the door whooshed open. Gritting my teeth against the pain, I turned my head, and opened my eyes to see Queen Solanta enter the room, followed by two Atan guards and a meek-looking Orna.

"Good morning, Prince Llyskel," Queen Solanta said cheerfully as she approached the bed. "Welcome to Atan. I was sorry to hear about your little mishap on the way here. A concussion, my healers tell me, but they assure me that with plenty of bed rest, you'll be fine in no time."

"Where is Neia?"

"Who?"

"Neia, my guard. She was with me—"

"You came alone, Prince Llyskel."

Came alone? I frowned. So, they had left her behind. If only I could be certain that meant Neia was all right, that they hadn't hurt or killed her, and that she'd been able to tell Father and Ariv what happened to me.

Ariv, who would be waiting for me at the gate. But I wouldn't be there. I had let Atan soldiers ambush me—who else would do Queen Solanta's bidding?—had let my obsession with shooters get the better of me. I had let Ariv down.

Queen Solanta sat on the edge of my bed and smiled at me. "We're already preparing the ball in honour of your visit and the upcoming betrothal. Orna is quite delighted."

I frowned and looked at Orna, who didn't even look up from the floor. So much for being delighted. As for the queen… I couldn't understand. She had had me abducted, yet here she was, talking to me as if I travelled here for a voluntary visit. And what was this betrothal? What did it mean?

"I'll have one of the cooks bring up some broth for you. I've been told you need rest, so I'll not keep you long." Queen Solanta rose and righted her skirts. "Rest well, Prince Llyskel. I'm looking forward to seeing you dance with Orna at the ball."

When Orna moved to follow her mother, Queen Solanta turned to her, shaking her head. "No. You stay. Get to know him."

Orna flinched when the door closed. She didn't move and stood with her back turned to me, watching the door.

"This betrothal," I asked her. "Is that an Atan celebration?"

Orna's head shot up, and she turned around. "You don't know?"

"No."

Orna looked at the bed and back at the door. She took a few steps and stopped. "It's when two people promise to wed."

Wed, that meant marriage. It sounded like a betrothal was like a courtship. "And who will be betrothed?"

Orna shook her head.

"You don't know?"

Orna shook her head again.

"You do know."

This time, Orna nodded.

That didn't make sense. Unless… "You don't want to tell me."

A shake again.

"Why not?"

Orna bit her lip. "Mother told me not to."

It had to be the concussion, because it took a while before it dawned on me what that could mean. "I'm one of the betrothed, aren't I?"

Wide golden eyes locked onto mine, even as Orna said, "No."

She was lying, though I wished she weren't. Abducted to marry me off to… to whom? Vik or… No. Orna was a mere stripling, a shy stripling who could barely stand to dance with a man. "Why?"

"I will be fifteen in six moons, and Mother thinks you'd be a suitable consort for me."

Though the answer came quickly this time, it sounded as if rehearsed, and Orna looked anything but happy about it. A sentiment I shared. Me, a suitable consort for a stripling girl? Was the queen mad? I was already being courted. Of course, the queen probably didn't know about that.

"It's our way," Orna continued. "When a girl reaches that age, her parents find her a suitable, mature husband, to guide her and father her offspring."

Those words coming out of Orna's mouth made me shudder. She couldn't seriously be expected to raise a family at this age. Let alone with me. "Why me?"

That seemed to startle Orna. Though, honestly, anything seemed to startle her. "Because of your… because you…"

It was suddenly painfully clear to me what Orna was too embarrassed to say; her eyes said it for her. Queen Solanta thought I was a perfect consort for Orna because I was the fifth son, the powerless Prince of Eizyrr. I remembered what my parents had said about Royal Consort Rass. "No rights," Mother had said. He had no rights aside from those Queen Solanta granted him. The queen wanted me because I had no powers. I couldn't even leave this room, as the door and windows opened with magic. I had a feeling the queen wouldn't be amenable to making the castle more accessible to me once I wed her daughter.

I swallowed and clenched my fists to quench my anger. This wasn't Orna's fault. "Why abduct me? She could have petitioned for me during your visit." I knew the answer even before I finished asking the question. Queen Solanta's request would have been declined. My parents had refused to let me visit Atan to paint; they weren't going to be open to a petition to wed their daughter. Especially now that Ariv was courting me. "I'm not going to do it."

"You have to."

"Do you want to be wed to me?"

"No!" Orna shrank back as she said it, eyes wide with fear.

I smiled at her and hoped she didn't think I was angry at her. "It's all right to feel that way." How could I blame her? I didn't want to be wed to her, either.

"No. Mother said you're to be my consort. She said… she said…"

I could well imagine what Queen Solanta had said. She would expect Orna to do as she was told. I closed my eyes. I couldn't expect Orna to go against her mother's wishes, her mother's command. It was up to me to try and stop this betrothal.

—∞—

I SPENT THE next two days sleeping and planning. Though less planning than sleeping, unfortunately. Orna kept visiting me, and there were times I thought being betrothed to her wouldn't be such a bad thing. It would keep Queen Solanta happy and Orna away from being betrothed to the next best potential consort in line.

I only had to think of Ariv to stop myself from giving in to those thoughts. There was nothing I wanted more than be back with him. I closed my eyes and imagined Ariv as he trained with me, his suntanned skin glistening with sweat, his eyes locked on mine, a hint of promise in them. How his strong arms would wrap around me as he kissed me, how they would pull on the rope he bound me with…

The door opened, and I jerked, head throbbing, making sure I was completely covered. Orna approached my bed and sat on the edge. I pushed the thoughts of Ariv down as I willed my body to relax into the bed. I wanted to go home. Still, looking at Orna, I wished I could take her with me, at least until Vik and Royal Consort Rass returned from their trip. A trip I had no doubt had been planned by Queen Solanta to keep them away.

"No sign of Vik or Father," Orna said, sounding disappointed.

I wasn't surprised. Orna was convinced that Vik would talk Queen Solanta out of the betrothal. He had already told her to wait to find Orna a consort, that Orna was too young to be betrothed. I had no doubt Vik would try again, but abducting me seemed a clear sign that the queen had no intention of listening to her son. In any case, I didn't think Vik and his father would be back in time to stop the betrothal.

That was why I'd decided to make a run for it as soon as I could. If only my plan worked.

"Tell me more about the gardens, Orna."

"Oh, the merus flowers are blooming near the south gate. They're yellow and orange with large dark green stems. They smell like honey. Or honey smells like merus flowers. I can't remember what the gardener said." She glowed. "Have you ever seen a merus flower?"

I shook my head and listened carefully for any hint of a layout of the gardens. It was hard to form a clear picture, but I knew I needed to keep away from the south gate she kept talking about. Orna mentioned a smaller gate to the west, once, but nothing about guards. Still, that gate would seem safer for me to get through. Less crowded.

Orna had already told me all I needed to know about the layout of the castle. Even if I didn't have a complete image, I knew I'd be able to find my way around. I hoped that one day she would forgive me for using her this way.

As soon as Orna left, I would get out of bed and look out of the window to confirm what she told me. My head still throbbed, but concussion or not, I only had one day left before the ball. If I didn't get out of bed now, I might as well give up.

I HATED THE tunic, trousers, and thin leather shoes I'd been presented with. I put them on, of course—running away in a sleeping gown would be madness—but the colours were far too bright to be inconspicuous, and the shoes weren't meant to be worn on long walks.

Orna had left a little while ago, and I felt a pang of regret for leaving her behind. I hoped her faith in Vik was well-founded, and that he would keep her safe from the queen's plans. There was nothing I could do for her, short of wedding her myself, and I was not going to let that happen.

The doors were almost as thick as the walls, but through

the cracks I could hear slivers of chatter coming from downstairs. The guests were arriving for dinner. Just a little longer and I'd be gone.

I waited until the voices died down, assuming they had all been led to the dining room. I didn't know exactly where that was, but there was at least one hall between the entrance and the dining room. I hoped that meant the entrance was free, because I didn't fancy jumping down from the balcony. Too big a risk of breaking bones. Not to mention having to smash a window to get to the balcony. Bloody magical doors.

Getting out of bed was less challenging than I'd expected. Until lunch time, I had still felt light-headed every time I sat up. I had no idea what the queen's healer had given me, but I could barely even feel my head throb any more, which was a good sign. I hoped it would last.

The day before, my plan had been to tear my tunic and ask the guard outside my door for help, hitting him as soon as he came in. And then I'd been told I could walk to the toilets by myself. This solved the problem of having to run around with a torn tunic, as well as the indignity of a bedpan.

All I had to do now was knock and tell the guard I needed to go to the toilet. It seemed so simple, yet I couldn't bring myself to do it. I stood in front of the door, staring at it, willing it to open on its own. Despite Ariv's lessons, I was afraid I would miss or not punch the guard hard enough.

When I had finally gathered enough courage to knock, the door opened immediately. The guard had barely taken one step into the room, when I raised my hands, pulled the right one back and punched him...in his shoulder. He opened his mouth, but I quickly followed up with my left, hitting him in the jaw this time. My hands hurt, but the guard staggered back and fell against the wall next to the door, hard. I stared at him as he slid to the ground. I'd done it. I had actually knocked the

guard out. And then the door started sliding shut.

I barely made it out of the room before it closed. With my back against the wall, I listened for footsteps or voices, but heard nothing. My footsteps barely made any sound, thanks to the rough leather soles, and I leaned over the railing to see if there were any guards downstairs. There didn't seem to be any, and I hurried down the large staircase.

Trying to remember as much of the layout as I could, I turned towards a dark corridor that would lead to a small side entrance. The servants' entrance. The front door would have been easier, but those were bound to be guarded.

The servants' entrance was close to the kitchen, and if Queen Solanta's servants were anything like our own, they would leave that side entrance propped open, so they could sneak out for a quick smoke without anyone hearing the door. If not, I'd have to wait for the servants to open it.

I shuffled through the corridor, staying in the dark, ready to hide should someone come my way. As I neared the kitchen, I heard loud voices amongst the clatter of pots and pans, and my heart pounded as I crept around the corner, but the kitchen door was closed. As was the side entrance. I pushed against it, hoping it wasn't latched, that they left it open just a smidge for easier access, but it didn't budge. So much for getting out the easy way.

Finding a spot where I couldn't be easily seen from either side of the corridor, I pressed my back against the wall and waited.

It took a while for one of the servants to appear. As tempted as I was to run after her when she went outside, I didn't. I counted the time between her exiting and the door closing again, and again when the servant came back in and disappeared into the kitchen. My best shot was when someone came back in, just before the kitchen door opened for them.

They'd be turned away from me for a short while. If I waited too long, the kitchen door would be open, light would flood the corridor, and anyone would be able to see me.

I didn't have to wait long before another servant entered the corridor and went outside. I clenched my hands to keep them from trembling as I waited for him to come back. By the time the servant came back in, my nails were pressed deep into my palms and all I could think of was sprinting across the gardens until I reached the nearest wall.

He walked more slowly than the woman had, and if I didn't go now, I'd have to wait for the next one. With one last look at the man, I pushed myself off the wall and sprinted towards the door. I made it outside, but didn't dare look back to check whether I'd been seen. I had to run. I had to make it to the wall before I could stop. There would be nowhere to hide, nothing but grass and low flowerbeds, until I reached that wall.

Noises came from behind me, or perhaps from somewhere to the side. I didn't know who or what made those noises, but I couldn't stop, not until I finally reached the wall and could duck behind the bushes.

Whatever that healer had given me seemed to be wearing off. My head pounded as I rested on hands and knees to catch my breath. Only when I could manage the pain did I dare peek through the bushes. I noticed something at the back of the castle, but no one moved towards me, and I sat back against the wall in relief. I had made it.

Of course, this was only the inner wall.

Chapter Eight

I HADN'T DARED ask Orna about guards, but I had expected there to be more in the outer gardens. The soldiers' quarters were all on the east side, at least, but I expected to see them guarding the entrances, even those of the inner wall. I crawled towards the narrow opening in the inner wall that would lead to a large walled-in garden with a fountain. Now and then, I stopped to peer at the servants' entrance. Not that anyone would be able to see me, but I felt better for checking.

There were no guards near the opening, and I slipped into the fountain garden without trouble. There were more openings in the wall, on both the south and north side of the garden, and I made my way to the north side, sticking close to the wall.

The fountain was as lovely as Orna had made it sound. The marble bridge across it, carved to look like wood, had been done beautifully, and I liked how the water flowed off the sides. Most of all, I loved the statues of the water nymphs sitting on top of the bridge, looking as if they were splashing water at each other. Whoever made it was clearly as fond of water nymphs as I was, and in other circumstances, I would have loved to paint the fountain.

Painting. That was what had got me here. No, that wasn't true. Queen Solanta didn't want me for my painting skills, she wanted me for my lack of magic.

When I reached the opening, I leaned my head back against the wall and closed my eyes, waiting for my head to stop throbbing. When I'd overheard my parents talk about not allowing me to go to Atan, I had wanted to show them I wasn't as helpless as they thought. This wasn't quite what I'd had in mind. I could barely believe that only a couple of days ago, I had been in the forest painting Neia at the waterfall, and now I was trying to escape a queen intent on betrothing me to her daughter. My parents were never going to let me out of their sight again.

I cautiously peered through the opening. Dark shadows surrounding the castle kept me from seeing much, but there didn't seem to be any guards near. I ran to the first tree, the second, third. I could see a little farther now, could see movement down the garden. I hoped it was just the wind playing with the leaves of a tree.

Keeping my eyes on whatever was moving, I made it to the fourth tree and the fifth, only to freeze as a voice rang out behind me.

"Prince Llyskel? What are you doing in our gardens?"

I rounded the tree and peered at the speaker from behind it. Prince Vik, flanked by Royal Consort Rass. I had no idea where they had come from. Had they been behind me all along? What should I do? I looked behind me. Nothing but the same movement, which had to be a tree. I couldn't see the east gate yet, but I couldn't stay here, so I ran.

Vik cursed, and both of them called after me, but I kept running until I finally saw the gate, and froze. Guards. They didn't seem to have seen me yet, so I slipped behind a tree, even though that put me in full view of Vik and Consort Rass. I looked around, desperate for another way out. So close, I'd been so close, and now I was trapped.

As I turned around to face Vik and Consort Rass, my head started pounding again. Barely noticeable at first, but louder, harder, with every step they took towards me, with every breath I took. I leaned back against the tree as I tried to get my breathing under control, tried to keep from throwing up when the pain became unbearable, tried to keep from sliding to the ground.

A sudden commotion behind me caused Vik and Consort Rass to stop, but I didn't look around. I knew I would fall if I even thought about it. So I stayed still and waited for the guards to reach me and take me back inside.

"What..." Vik started to say, but he wasn't looking at me.

A hand touched my arm, and I jerked, tried to pull away, and turned my head too fast. My vision turned black around the edges as I saw the face I loved close in on me. I smiled, or tried to, and let Ariv pull me against him. My stomach turned at the movement, but Ariv's warmth, his familiar scent, made up for the queasy feeling.

I looked into his eyes, feeling my knees buckle, and was glad Ariv was strong enough to keep me from falling.

"I knocked out a guard," I told him as my world blacked out.

MY HEAD HURT. It was throbbing, following the rhythm of my heartbeat, and I wished it would stop. I couldn't think. There was something in the back of my mind, something about Vik and Consort Rass chasing me. Ariv had been there as well. He rescued me. Had I been dreaming?

The pillow smelled familiar, of home, and Ariv.

I opened my eyes and sighed in relief. The image was a bit fuzzy, but I could clearly see green walls. *My* green walls. I was in my own room. I closed my eyes again. Not a dream.

"Good morning, sleepyhead."

I didn't open my eyes, but reached out until my hand was caught by Ariv's strong, warm grip, and sighed again.

"So, knocked out a guard, huh?"

"Yes," I whispered hoarsely. My mouth was dry, and I smacked my lips.

Something was pressed to my lips, a cloth, a moist cloth. I sucked at it, enjoying the cool water as it wet my mouth.

"You rescued me." I remembered now.

"Of course."

"The queen wanted to betroth me to Orna." Orna. I needed to go back. Someone needed to go back and save Orna. I tried to lift my head, only to be pressed back into the bed.

"Stay still, you idiot. You have a concussion."

"Orna. She's too young. I…"

"Princess Orna is safe."

"Promise?"

"Promise. The queen has stepped down, and King Vik has taken the crown. We received word this morning."

"Stepped down?" It couldn't have been that easy.

"Well, that's the official version." Ariv lowered his voice. "But I overheard your brothers saying King Vik gave her no choice."

That made more sense. I frowned. This morning? "How long have I been home?" It was strange to think of Vik as the king of Atan, but it made me feel a lot better for Orna, knowing Vik would look after her.

"Two days."

Two days. The memories seemed too fresh for that. So did the pain in my head. "But I was healing. I didn't feel any pain after the queen's healer gave me something for my concussion."

Ariv snorted, but it sounded off. "Of course you didn't. What that healer gave you may have numbed your pain, but it didn't heal the concussion. And your escape attempt only aggravated it. You shouldn't have been on your feet at all. You've been in and out of consciousness for the past two days." Ariv's hand tightened around mine.

I opened my eyes to look at him. As much as I loved my room, the green seemed to dance in front of my eyes, and I could barely even see Ariv. I blinked. He dimmed the light, but his face remained blurry. I reached out with my free hand. Ariv caught it and held it against his cheek as he moved his face closer to mine. I could see his eyes now, tinged with concern. Ariv was worried, had been worried. "Was it that bad?"

"Yes. You wouldn't wake up at first."

"I'm sorry."

"Not your fault."

"But it is."

"Llyskel—"

"I saw the shooters, Ariv. I saw them, and I froze. I…" I closed my eyes. I didn't want to see Ariv's disappointment. I should have ducked, run, jumped into the water. I should have done something. "I did nothing. I could have escaped, but I just kept staring at those shooters and did nothing."

When Ariv let go of my hand, I expected him to go, but he didn't. He caressed my cheek and sighed. "There were three of them, Neia told us. You were ambushed. They weren't going to let you run away."

"But I could have tried!"

Ariv put a finger against my lips. "You sound like Neia. She hasn't stopped blaming herself, not even when we got you back."

"How is Neia?" I asked, liking the way Ariv's finger brushed my lips as I spoke.

"She's fine. Angry and slightly bruised, but fine. She was there, you know, when we came to get you."

I remembered only Ariv. "I felt powerless," I confessed. And I hated it. "All my life I've been sheltered, but I never felt that powerless before. Frustrated, but never as powerless as when I saw those shooters and couldn't stop myself from reacting."

"Neia told us she saw you fall like you were stunned. So, you didn't do 'nothing'. You adapted."

I opened my mouth to speak, but closed it when it dawned on me that Ariv was right. I *had* done something.

"When Neia told us that, I knew that you'd be fine. That you'd find a way to protect yourself until we could get to you," Ariv said as he trailed his finger across my bottom lip, following it with a kiss.

I shuddered as his dry, warm lips touched mine. I'd missed him, missed his touch, and I wanted more. It didn't take much to drag his body on top of mine, and he came willingly. Though I could feel him, he managed to keep his weight off me. I pushed my body into his as he deepened the kiss, burying my hands in his short hair. It wasn't enough. Pushing, pulling, it didn't matter what I tried, Ariv wouldn't budge. Worse, he drew back completely.

"No…" I grabbed at him.

Ariv shook his head. "We can't."

"I need you."

Ariv swallowed. "I know what you need. But I can't give it to you now. You need to heal first."

He was right. Of course he was right, but that didn't mean I had to like it. "Don't go."

A quick peck on my lips, and Ariv was stretching himself

out next to me, lying on his side, his head close to mine. "Not going anywhere."

I wriggled even closer and entwined my fingers with his, moving our hands to rest on my stomach, and closed my eyes.

—∞—

FOUR MORE DAYS of bed rest, and I felt the walls closing in on me. My head had finally stopped hurting, and I had been allowed to sit up for small stretches, but not to walk or go outside. Not until now.

I sat on the balcony, easel in front of me, paintbrush in my hand, watching Sirr play in the garden. She knew I was here and kept looking up, pointing, calling out, telling me what she was doing. She seemed less restless, less out of control, but Inau feared more outbursts were to come. For now, she enjoyed watching her daughter play with only the minimal shielding needed.

Inau sat on a low bench next to the annex, leaning back against the wall, exactly as I was painting her. It felt like my first painting—new, awkward. I couldn't get from line to brushstroke, at first, couldn't get my hands to move the way I wanted them to. It was like learning to paint all over again.

Halfway through the painting, I seemed to regain my flow. My movements were more fluent, I didn't have to think what to do next, and I could breathe again. The painting looked all right now. It was not my best work, but not my worst either, merely...different. Inau looked beautifully relaxed, with her face soaking up the sun's rays, a soft smile playing around her lips as she watched her daughter play. Carefree.

"You captured her well."

Just that voice was enough to make me shudder. Four days since I woke up, and I was itching for him to take me.

Hands rested on my shoulders, and I felt their warmth spread through my body.

"You're early."

"Yes. We finished clearing these fields. We start on the last two fields tomorrow."

Plenty of time to play, then. I grabbed Ariv's hands and rose. Ariv nodded and led me back into my room and up the stairs, walking backwards until he reached my bed. The rope and shooter lay on the covers. *Yes.* I shivered. *Yes, please.*

Ariv grinned at my reaction. He opened his mouth to speak, but I kissed him instead. No more talking. There was no talking when we undressed each other, dropping clothes left and right, and no talking when we kissed each other again until we were both breathless, not even when he grabbed the rope and started binding me.

I couldn't take my eyes off him as he knotted the rope in place, couldn't stop shivering and moaning as he trailed his fingers over my skin next to the rope. It felt so good.

When he was done, I expected him to push me back onto the bed, but he didn't. Instead, he kneeled in front of me and blew puffs of air across my cock, looking straight into my eyes, a grin on his lips. I let my head fall back and was glad Ariv was holding onto my hips or I would have fallen. When he licked my cock from root to top, I bit my lip to keep from screaming. The balcony doors were still open, and I didn't want Inau and Sirr to hear me.

Moist warmth enveloped my cock as Ariv took me into his mouth and I groaned, pushing my hips forward, wanting more. Ariv's hold on my hips prevented me from reaching my goal, however, his movements slow and teasing. I shuddered and moaned with every swipe of his tongue, with every scratch of his teeth.

"Please," I begged as I looked down at him, but Ariv just

winked, looking beautiful with his wetted lips around my cock.

I closed my eyes as he sucked. I opened my mouth, but there were no words for the way he made me feel.

Suddenly, Ariv's mouth left my cock, his hands released my hips, and when I opened my eyes, he stood before me, aiming his shooter at me. Mouth still open, I shivered, unable to look away from it. My body reacted instantly, and my muscles pulled taut against the rope.

"Gorgeous," Ariv whispered. "So inviting, so open."

Ariv's hand on the shooter was as strong as I remembered, and I wanted him to stun me, wanted to smell lingering scent of his spell as he fucked me.

"Your expression is so easy to read. I knew what you wanted when I caught you out in the forest. The way you looked at my shooter. The way your eyes followed it like they are now. I wanted to have you."

I tore my eyes away from the shooter and looked at Ariv, his eyes dark and full of desire.

"But I knew even before that. You never saw me looking at you as you painted them, the shooters, the hands. Back when you were still too mortified to admit what you wanted. So young, so open... It was hard to stay away from you."

He had always known. Was I that obvious?

Ariv shook his head, and I realised I'd asked it out loud.

"*They* don't know what to look for." He moved his hand, and I was drawn to his shooter again. "Llyskel."

I looked up, slowly, my eyes not leaving the shooter until the last possible moment. Ariv didn't say a word, but merely grinned.

"What?" I asked.

"That's twice, now."

I frowned. Twice, what? Ariv's question made no sense, not until he held up his shooter and hid it behind his back. Then

I glared at him. He was testing me. I thought he was teasing me with his chatter, but he was testing me, and looking far too pleased with himself.

"Don't pout," he said. "You needed to know you could do it, could resist the pull of the shooter."

He was right, again. With the shooter behind his back, it was easier to concentrate on him, and I looked into his eyes. "Did you mean what you said?"

He stepped up to me, wrapping his free arm around me as he kissed me, quick and demanding. "All of it."

A bit dazed, I leaned into him, resting my head against his shoulder. "Good."

I could feel Ariv grin as he kissed my neck, right before he pushed me onto the bed, pulled the shooter from behind his back, and pointed it at me. The rope pulled against my skin as I froze, staring at his hand holding the shooter. His fingers clenched around the handle. I could barely wait for the zing of the shooter, the scent of magic, and Ariv's hands on my body.

Epilogue

I T FELT GOOD to get back into my training routine—running laps, practising my stance, my punches, learning kicks and rolls and feints—even if I tired more quickly than I had before. I was soaking with sweat when we finished and ready to take a midday nap.

"You should," Ariv said when I complained about it. He pulled me against him and held my wrists, rubbing his thumbs across the fading lines of the rope. I pushed my hips against his, and Ariv grinned. "Later. I promise." He kissed me. "I need to go."

I didn't want him to leave, but Ariv shook his head and pushed me towards the showers. "Go shower. And take that nap."

I would rather take a nap with him. I turned to tell him that, but Ariv was already walking away. He turned when he reached the doorway, and as the sunlight glinted off his well-toned shoulders, I remembered wanting to paint him like this, leaning against the sunlit doorway, shooter hanging loosely from his hand, looking strong and gorgeous. I stared at him as I waited for him to disappear, memorising the pose. He didn't. He just stood there and looked at me.

Before I knew it, Ariv was back at my side again, wrapping his arms around me, sighing. "Stop looking at me like that, I really need to go." He kissed me again, the barest brush of his lips, before resting his forehead against mine. "Meet me at the gate at the dinner bell," he whispered as he pulled away from me.

Fingers against my lips, I pushed down the thought of what happened last time he uttered those words to me and focussed on the sliver of excitement coursing through me. We were finally going out together as a couple and let the world see that I was his.

Ariv grabbed my wrist. A spark shone in his dark eyes as he put his lips to the fading rope marks. My breath hitched and shivers—memories, anticipation—shot through my body.

"Be a good prince, and don't let anyone abduct you today. Mum's expecting us for dinner." Ariv winked and walked off. "She insists on meeting the one who managed to tie me down."

Acknowledgements

A big thanks to:

My critters—Anne, Jordan, JRose, Kaje, Kari, LC, and Taylor—for helping me iron out the kinks,

Josh, for the beta and the fresh insight,

Simoné, for the gorgeous cover art,

Yana Goya, for the wonderful illustrations,

KJ Charles, for the editing, and for making me hate the term 'first date' :p

Tami Veldura, for the proofreading, and catching a bunch of unchecked turnings and pullings ;),

Meredith Bond, for reminding me how much fun coding can be with her self-publishing course,

Kari, Josh, and Aleks, for being there for me,

Jarsto, Dorinde, and Jasper, for putting up with me asking the strangest—mostly out of context—questions, and answering them,

My Men, for supporting me.

About the Author

Blaine D. Arden is a purple-haired, forty-something author of gay & trans* romance mixed with fantasy, mystery, and magic who sings her way through life in platform boots.

Born and raised in Zutphen, the Netherlands, Blaine spent many hours of her sheltered youth reading, day dreaming, making up stories and acting them out with her Barbies. After seeing the film *"An Early Frost"* as a teen in the mid-eighties, an idealistic Blaine wanted to do away with the negativity surrounding homosexuality and strove to show the world how beautiful love between men could be. *Our difference is our strength*, is Blaine's motto, and her stories are often set in worlds where gender fluidity and sexual diversity are accepted as is.

Blaine has been published by Storm Moon Press, Less Than Three Press, and Wilde City Press. Her scifi romance *"Aliens, Smith and Jones"* received an Honourable Mention in the Best Gay Sci-Fi/Fantasy category of the Rainbow Awards 2012.

For more information about Blaine and her books, visit her website: http://blainedarden.com

Also by Blaine D. Arden

Aliens, Smith and Jones

<u>Anthologies</u>
Carved in Flesh
Legal Briefs (charity anthology)
Sweethearts and Seduction
Project Fierce Chicago (charity anthology)
Bedtime Stories
Satisfaction Guaranteed

<u>Freebies</u>
Color Me
The Storyteller
Slippery When Wet
An Invitation to Love

<u>Coming in 2015</u>
The Forester: a Triad in Three Acts

Printed in Great Britain
by Amazon